The
FOX GIRL
and the
WHITE
GAZELLE

For Maws and Martin,
without whose support this book
could never have been written.

Kelpies is an imprint of Floris Books
First published in 2018 by Floris Books
© 2018 Victoria Williamson

Victoria Williamson asserts her right under the
Copyright, Designs and Patents Act 1988 to be
recognised as the Author of this Work

The publisher acknowledges subsidy from
Creative Scotland towards the publication
of this volume.

MIX
Paper from
responsible sources
FSC® C117931

Also available as an eBook

British Library CIP Data available
ISBN 978-178250-490-0
Printed & bound by MBM Print SCS Ltd, Glasgow

The FOX GIRL
and the
WHITE GAZELLE

VICTORIA WILLIAMSON

The Fox

Growls in the dark: the monsters are coming,
Tearing the earth with their terrible teeth.
 Engine-roar, rubber-burn, metal mouths shrieking.
  Closer, closer, closer they crawl.

   My den is collapsing, roof caving, walls crumbling.
   I race up the tunnel before I am trapped.
   My dog mate is dead and I am alone now.
   My green haven ruined, my home turned to dust.

   A flash in the dark. A monster has caught me!
   A crunching of metal and screeching of wheels.
  Bone-snapping, pain-burning, red life-blood flowing.
   My body is broken, and I am afraid.

   I pick myself up but my limp leg is useless.
   Whimper-crawl, stumble-drag under a fence.
   My belly is heavy, the young ones will come soon.
    Here I must stay till they grow big and strong.

     But this is not home.
     It hurts, it hurts.
     No, this is not home.
     It *hurts*.

1
Caylin

The home-time bell's so loud it hurts my head. I clamp one hand over my ear and stuff my pencil case and books back in my bag with the other. Everyone else rushes for the door, but I take my time. I'm in no hurry. 6B next door had PE last thing, and that girl with the blonde ponytail won't be finished changing for another five minutes. When she gets down to the alley behind the hairdressers I'll be waiting for her.

But not because I'm her friend.

It's her birthday today. She was walking round the playground with a big 'Happy 11th Birthday' badge on like a Disney princess on parade. I mean, how stupid can you get? Talk about an open invitation.

Not to her actual party, of course. I haven't had one of those special pink envelopes filled with glitter from anyone for years. I don't care though. I don't need friends. And I don't need an invitation from Zoe Snot-Nosed Weir to the kind of party where I knock the sugar-filled stuffing out of her.

It's not a pretty pink invitation I want from her anyway.

It's her birthday money I'm after.

I zip up my bag and put my jacket on slowly, staring out of the window at the Drumhill estate. It looks just like the cardboard model on the display table, only our cornflake-box tower blocks are painted blue instead of boring grey like the real thing, and Mrs Gibb made us hang a sparkly yellow sun above them. Ha! That's a joke. It's only just stopped raining outside, and if I'm not careful my feet'll be soaking by the time I splash through the puddles to Grandad's house for—

Oh.

Then I remember, and my knees turn to wobbly jelly. It's been over a year since the accident and I still forget sometimes: I can't go to Grandad's house ever again.

I squeeze my hands into fists and stare out at the grey sky, trying to pretend that I don't care and the lump in my throat doesn't hurt me at all.

"Caylin?" my teacher calls. "Are you still here?"

No, I'm not. You're hallucinating. Maybe you're mad. Stupid old witch.

Mrs Gibb comes back into the classroom and interrupts my daydreams. She's always doing that. I'm pretty sure the thought of telling me off is what gets her out of bed in the morning.

"Didn't you hear the bell?"

The whole of Glasgow heard the bell Mrs Gibb. It's probably set about a hundred decibels over the safety limit.

I know all about decibels. There was a programme on the other night about noise pollution and why so many kids are going deaf. From now on I'll be covering my ears every time they try to wreck our hearing with that school bell of theirs. I don't want to end up half-deaf like Mrs Mitchell in the flat downstairs.

Mrs Gibb says I watch too much TV, but I learn more from the telly than I do from her stupid lessons about fractions and decimals. Who cares what you get when you multiply a bit of one thing with a bit of something else? All you end up with is still just bits. That's what my life is like now. Bits multiplied by bits adding up to a whole heap of broken nothing.

Try to work that sum out on your blackboard Mrs Gibb. I dare you.

"Caylin, are you listening? It's time to go home."

Mrs Gibb is sighing now, and that's one of her warning signs.

I don't answer, but I pick up my bag and head for the door. I'm only halfway there when she stops me.

"Look Caylin, we need to talk."

Make up your mind.

I stare at my feet and fiddle with my backpack straps so she'll know I'm not interested in anything she's going to say.

"I don't have time today, I'm running late for a meeting, but perhaps one day next week your mother could pop in for a quick chat after school? Would that be possible?"

My jaw clenches, my hands gripping my backpack straps tightly now for support. I swallow hard, trying to remember just one of the million excuses I've invented to explain why no one ever sees Mum any more. The lies all disappear down a deep dark hole right when I need them most, and the fear of being found out is all they leave behind.

"I'll ask her," I mumble. My throat is dry as sawdust, and I wince at the way the 's' comes out as a 'th'. I hate my lisp. I hate talking. And I hate Mrs Gibb for making me talk.

"Sorry?" Mrs Gibb says.

I glower at her, half-angry, half-afraid. She heard exactly what I said. She always makes me repeat myself and look stupid in class.

"I'll ask her," I repeat, just as quietly as before, praying Mrs Gibb will give up and stop asking about Mum.

"You really will have to speak up and stop mumbling," Mrs Gibb sighs, focusing all her unwanted attention on my speech impediment instead. "You're nearly twelve and you're starting high school this year. I know you're self-conscious about your lisp, but with a bit of daily practice I'm sure—"

"Got to go. I'm late," I growl, not caring whether the old witch hears me or not.

I hurry past her, practically running down the corridor to the main doors. Everything Mrs Gibb says makes me want to scream. Why does she always have to talk about my lisp like it's the only thing that matters about me? My face is burning with embarrassment. The thought of her trying to set up a meeting with Mum and noticing our phone's been cut off, or worse, dropping by one day after school, makes my throat so tight I can barely breathe. What if she finds out about Mum and then—

Don't think about it! Only a few more months and then I'll be out of here and away from Mrs Gibb and her stupid questions for good.

Only a few more months and then I'll be starting high school.

My stomach knots, and I want to throw up right there in the playground.

Primary school's bad enough, even with me being bigger and meaner than all the other kids who'd snigger at me behind their hands if I gave them half a chance. What'll happen when I start a new school as the scabby wee first-year with the lisp and the cheap clothes who never has money for school trips? How will I keep my secrets safe then?

Maybe I'll just run away. Maybe I'll keep running and never come back.

But not today. Today I have a job to do.

I walk out the gates and take a good look round. I've timed it just right. The parents picking up the younger kids have gone and the groups of girls chatting on their mobiles and boys kicking footballs have moved on. The street's almost empty. No witnesses.

Perfect.

2
Reema

The man in the wheelchair is having a fit. He is jerking and shaking, and there is a line of drool running down his chin. A group of people is gathering at the entrance of the temporary accommodation where my family has been staying. They want to help, but they do not know what to do, so they just stand there and stare at us. I am so ashamed I want to wrap my headscarf right over my face so they cannot see me.

"Is Baba alright Reema?" Sara asks, clutching my hand tightly. My little sister is only seven, and our father's seizures frighten her just as much as the bombs and bullets of the endless war we escaped.

"He is fine," I lie, trying to sound confident. "It will be over soon."

"I wish Jamal was here," Sara sniffs. "He always knows what to do."

"Sshh!" I hiss, squeezing her hand much harder than I mean to. "Do not say his name so loud. You know how much it upsets Mama and Baba to hear it."

I wish more than anything that our brother Jamal was here too, but I have learned the hard way not to wish for the impossible.

"Reema! Stop daydreaming and come and help me with your father's chair," Mama calls.

Baba's fit is over and the audience has melted away as quickly as it gathered. I am relieved they are gone. We have only been in this country for two weeks, and already I am sick of the looks of pity and suspicion that follow us everywhere we go.

Mama is struggling to get Baba's wheelchair down the flight of steps. Karen, our helper from the Refugee Council, and Fatima the translator are trying to lift the front end of the heavy chair. Baba is exhausted by his seizure, but his jaw is clenched tight, and he is trying to pretend he does not care that he is being carried down to the street by three women instead of walking by himself.

He has been pretending a lot since the war began.

"Careful!" Mama warns as I drop the side I am carrying too soon. The small front wheel bumps down hard and Baba lurches forward, catching hold of the armrest to stop himself from falling. Even this small effort is difficult for him. He starts to cough, great choking wheezes that double him up and send shivers through his whole body.

I do not know what to do, so I take his hand and hold it tight, just like I do when my little sister is upset. It feels as though I am trying to hold my father together.

In my head I can still see Baba working in his car-repair shop back home in Aleppo, his arms as thick as tree trunks as he bends down to lift a tyre into place. In the picture in my mind, he turns to smile at me as I run into the workshop to tell him all about my day at school. He lifts me up, setting me on his broad shoulders and striding across the road to the café to buy me a slice of *harissa* cake.

He is big and strong, and even the impatient taxi drivers stop to let him pass. I sit on his knee in the shade of an olive tree outside as he orders us mint lemonade, his long beard tickling my ear until I am giggling so hard I can barely breathe. His own laugh is deep and booming, wrapping me up in a safe blanket of music and warmth.

And then the colour of the photo I am seeing starts to fade. Poison gas seeps into the image, curling the edges and shrivelling my father down to a pale shadow I barely recognise. His lungs and brain are damaged and his muscles have wasted away, until only the dark eyes staring back at me from the ruined picture in my mind are the same.

I have had a whole year to get used to the change, but still this thin person who shakes and coughs and fits seems like a stranger.

I want my real father back even more than I want to go home to Syria.

I rearrange the rug that has slipped from his frail legs, pretending I have not noticed that he soiled himself during his seizure. I cannot meet his eye. I have seen the shame there a thousand times over since the bombs destroyed our home and we fled, and even now the sight of his hurt makes me want to cry. He thinks he is useless now, broken. And all the oceans of tears I cry for him will not help me glue him back together again.

"Thanks *habibti*," he says softly, patting my hand and calling me 'my love' the way he used to when I was little.

My chest is tight and I look away quickly, feeling like the worst daughter in the world. I am scared in case he can see all of the things in my heart. I am terrified that one day he will find out that a tiny part of me is almost grateful for the terrible thing that happened to him. Only the most vulnerable refugee families who fled Syria were given the chance of a new life in another country. Without Baba's gas-choked lungs and damaged brain we would be spending years without hope in the refugee camp in Turkey.

Eight months of dust and hunger and cold was bad enough.

Suddenly an engine growls on the road behind me and I whirl round, my heart pounding.

Is it a tank? A truck full of soldiers?

No. It is just a car coming up the street. The red emergency light in my head switches off but my body does not relax.

"Sara, keep away from the road!" I shout at my sister, my concern for her making my voice sound harsh.

Sara skips back up onto the pavement and waves at the taxi driver. Her face is shining with excitement at the thought of moving house again, but she is only little and does not understand. She thinks the new place will be a permanent home, like the one we lost in Syria. But I am twelve, and I know better.

We do not belong here. We are refugees, and we will spend our lives moving from one place where we are not wanted to another.

The taxi driver gets out and helps us with Baba, smiling a gruff smile and saying things in English we do not understand. I look to Fatima for a translation, but it is clear she does not think his words are worth explaining. Fatima is a nice lady, but she has lived in this country all her life. This is her home. I do not think she really understands what it is like to feel overwhelmed by the newness of it all the way we do.

The taxi driver is friendly too, but I see the way he glances at the headscarves Mama and I are wearing. Even more than our second-hand clothes, these are what mark us out as foreign, different, *alien*. I know what he is thinking, how people here believe all Muslim women are covered up against their will and that I am far too young for this. I wish I could explain to him what this headscarf means to me. I wish I could tell him that this little scrap of cloth is all I have left of the country where I was born. One tiny fabric square – that is all I have to remind me of the bright-eyed boy who should be with us, who bought it for my birthday before the war.

We have not seen my brother Jamal since the night we fled Aleppo. I do not even know if he is dead or alive, and every time we move it feels as though I am travelling one step further away from him.

I am crying now without even knowing it, but as soon as Fatima sees she comes over and gives me a hug. "It is alright Reema," she says in Arabic. "There is not enough room in the taxi for all of us, but Karen is going to drive you to your new home. She will be right behind us all the way."

I shake my head. She thinks I am worried about being separated from my family. She does not understand, and it makes me cry harder.

"Are you sad to be leaving this house, is that it? I know you are disappointed not to be housed near the other Syrian families who flew to Glasgow with you, but you need somewhere that suits your father, Reema. Your new home is ready and waiting – it has an access ramp for your father's wheelchair, and your place at school has already been arranged. You will be happy here in Scotland, you will see."

None of these nice foreign people understand. Why does she keep calling this our home? Our home is Syria, and as soon as the war is over we are going back. We will rebuild our house, and things will be just like they used to be before the war came and ruined everything.

I want to yell this at the top of my voice, but instead I give her a watery smile and wave to Mama to show her I am alright. Baba is not the only one who is good at pretending. Mama's anxious frown relaxes and she gets into the taxi beside Baba with Fatima and Sara. I get into Karen's car, buckling up my seatbelt and trying not to bite my lip nervously every time we lose sight of the taxi in the heavy city traffic.

Karen points things out to me as we drive, and I repeat the unfamiliar words slowly, hesitantly, rolling them round on my tongue until I am used to the taste of them.

"Bank... Post Office... Supermarket... Motorway... Traffic lights... Canal... Drumhill... Flats..."

I gaze wide-eyed at the green of the fir trees, the grass, and the gardens with their colourful spring flowers. After the endless dust of war and the parched dirt of the refugee camp, I almost feel like I am drowning in green. Only the sky here is grey and the soft rain feels like tears on my cheeks.

"Look – park." Karen points, and when I follow her finger I see tall trees in rows by a fence. These are not fruit trees like the orchards on the outskirts of Aleppo, though. These trees are only just budding, but even when the leaves open there will be none of the tangerines and pears and plums that I remember from home.

Here even the trees speak a foreign language.

Karen stops the car, pointing to a three-storey building that looks like it contains six apartments. There is a path leading up to a wheelchair ramp and an open corridor that looks as though its entrance door was recently removed.

"This is it," Karen smiles. "Welcome home."

I understand her words this time, but she has got it all wrong.

This is not my home.

No.

This is not my home.

3
Caylin

I can see her coming down the path. Her blonde ponytail is swinging behind her, and there's a big smile on her smug wee face. I bet she's thinking about her birthday party and all the presents she's going to get.

I'm about to give her a present she won't forget in a hurry.

I wait till she's halfway down the alley, right behind the hairdressers, where no one can see her from the street. Then I step out from behind the bins and pull that shiny ponytail hard.

"Ow!" she yells. "Stop it! Let go!"

I shove her up against the wall and stare her right in the eye until she shuts up and starts shaking. I've done this enough times to know that's all I have to do. All of the kids at school know my reputation.

"Where is it?" I hiss, giving her a sharp poke in the ribs.

"What?" she whimpers, playing dumb. She knows what I'm after though, and her hand goes to her pocket to protect the purse inside.

"Give it to me." I grab her arm and twist it till she drops what she's holding. I pick up the sparkly purple purse and pull the crisp notes out. Fifteen pounds. More than I'd hoped for.

"Please Caylin!" she wails. "That's for my b-birthday!"

I'd tell her to shut up and stop snivelling, but there are too many 's's for me to say with my lisp without sounding stupid. I glare her into silence instead, pushing the notes deep into my bag and stuffing the empty purse back in her pocket, but I make the mistake of letting go of her too soon.

"I'm telling on you, Caylin Todd!" she yells. "I'm telling my mum and dad, and I'm telling the teachers, and the police, and—"

I shove her so hard she falls backwards onto the path. I learned long ago not to leave a mark that can be traced back to me.

It was Mum's last loser boyfriend, Rob, who taught me that.
Thanks Rob.

"You open your mouth you wee cow, and I'll kill you, get it?" I spit each word out like they're punching her in the gut. No 's's to trip over. It sounds like I mean it.

Zoe starts crying, big ugly sobs that send tears flooding down her cheeks. Her nose is running, and her hands are scraped from trying to break her fall. I stare at her for a long moment, and then I walk away. I know she's not going to tell anyone. She's too scared.

I break into a jog when I reach the park, heading for the corner shop down by the Chinese takeaway. I can't go to the Co-op store nearer school, I was only there a few days ago. It's always the same woman at the till, and she's started looking at me suspiciously when I put the week's shopping through.

She's wondering where my mum is too.

I'm starting to feel like the caribou calf I saw in that *Planet Earth* wildlife programme last weekend. It couldn't run fast enough from the wolf, and it got hunted down and separated from its mother.

I'm not going to let Social Services do that to me and Mum!

Before I know it I'm running so fast I'm chasing the wind through the park, the swings and slide lying abandoned as big drops of heavy rain begin to blow across the empty football field. I don't look up as I pass the climbing frame in the shape of a giant spider with outstretched legs. I'm not afraid of bugs, but Grandad's old house looks right onto the park, and if I turn my head now I'll see the familiar windows looking back at me over the fence. Another family lives there now. I don't belong there any more.

The memories hurt worse than ten million wooden skelfs sticking into my fingers, and I pump my legs harder, trying to outrun them. The ghosts of the past follow right behind me though, and I can hear Grandad's voice calling, "Look at that wee lassie go! She'll be running for Scotland one day, just like her gran!"

I used to love hearing him say that, telling me stories about my gran, the famous runner who died when I was still too young to remember. All I've got left of her are some old photos and the same frizzy hair that Mum and me share. The girls at school used to laugh when I boasted about her and said if she was so famous then how come they'd never heard of her? But I know she was. She ran for Scotland in the Commonwealth Games and had her picture in the paper and everything.

I don't talk about her now though.

I don't tell anyone anything any more.

There's a group of kids hanging around by the bus stop on the other side of the park, and I slow down to a jog. I don't want anyone seeing me running. They'd just make fun of me, even though it'd be a total scoosh to outrun the whole lot of them with a broken leg and a pair of crutches. There's no point being good at something if it just makes people laugh at you.

The kids aren't looking at me though, they're watching the bulldozers across the street digging up the wasteland to build a new community centre. Old Mrs Mitchell says it's about time, but it makes me sad to see the piles of dirt and stripped earth where there was once a sea of grass and wild flowers. There used to be rabbits in there too, and squirrels in the trees. One night on the way home from the cinema with Grandad I even saw the yellow eyes of a fox peering at me from behind the broken fence.

The foxes and rabbits and squirrels have nowhere to go now. Their homes have all been dug up and destroyed. That makes me feel almost as bad as the memories of losing Grandad's house, and before I know it the image of Zoe's tear-streaked face when she lost her birthday money is crowding into my head too and making me want to cry. Her crisp five-pound notes feel like they weigh a ton in my bag, but the guilt isn't enough to make me give them back.

I *need* them.

I haven't been to the corner shop for a few weeks now, and the man who runs it barely glances at me as I pay for the tins of beans and soup that I stuff into my backpack. When I'm done stocking up on toothpaste and toilet roll there's barely enough of Zoe's birthday money left to buy me and Mum chips for dinner.

I don't go to the chip shop near the high school though, I go to Michael's Superchippy further down, off the dual carriageway. There's always too many nosey old folk from my estate in the closer one to risk going in too often. Mrs Mitchell from downstairs is one of the regulars. After all the problems Mum's stupid ex-boyfriends have caused over the years, she'd just love an excuse to get rid of us from the flats for good.

The smell of frying makes my mouth water as I wait in the queue. I get free school lunches, but there wasn't anything in the cupboard for dinner last night and the cereal was finished three days ago. I gaze at the rows of fish and battered sausages longingly, but if I'm greedy there won't be enough money to get Mum chips too. She needs them more than me.

I have to think of Mum. She comes first.

I stuff the plastic bag with the wrapped chips down my jacket as soon as I get outside, hugging them to my chest and soaking up the warmth and delicious smell. Then I run home, the secret stash of chips protecting me from the wind and the rain like a magic charm. I don't care if my uniform stinks of grease tomorrow. I'll belt anyone who even mentions it.

I stop outside the entrance to our flats, suddenly wary.

Something's changed.

I don't like change. Change is never good.

The Wilsons and their kid in the wheelchair moved out a few days ago, but the access ramp the Council put in for him is still here and the door to their ground-floor flat opposite

Mrs Mitchell's is open. I walk up the ramp and into the close warily, wondering what mad bampots the Council will be dumping on us now.

Bampots.

I shouldn't use that word. Rob used it all the time, and he was the biggest bampot I've ever met.

There's a girl standing at the door of number 1A.

She's got eyes as big as dinner plates, Grandad's voice comes whispering in my ear. *But she's a wee skinny malinky longlegs!*

Get lost! I yell at the ghosts in my head, trying to focus on the girl instead. She's got cheap clothes on, and I can see strands of long black hair that have comes loose from under her green headscarf. She's holding a picture frame that doesn't have a photo in it, just a piece of paper with a whole bunch of squiggly writing that looks like a different language. I think she was about to hang the frame up on her hall wall when I stopped in her doorway.

We stare at one another for a long moment, sizing each other up. She's taller than me, but way skinnier. I could take her in a fight if I had to.

I can see she's waiting for me to speak. Everyone's always waiting for me to speak, to open my mouth and embarrass myself with my lisp. If she has something she wants to say then she can say it. I've got nothing to say to her. I was here first. She's on my territory.

The door behind me opens and Mrs Mitchell comes out, carrying a box of tea. She always takes new people tea when they move into the estate. She pretends she's being kind, but she's

22

really just a nosey old cow who tries to find out all their secrets so she can gossip about them down at her bingo club. She's nearly blind and has a bad knee that stops her getting about much, but she knows everything about everyone from one end of Drumhill to the other.

The thought of her finding out about Mum and phoning Social Services makes me break out in a cold sweat.

"Hello Caylin, you're back late from school. Where have you been?" She scowls at me through a big fake smile like she's worried I might've learned something about the new people before her. Then her eyes narrow and fix on the bulging backpack I'm trying to hide behind me. "What have you been up to? What have you got there?"

"Nothing," I mutter, backing away towards the stairs and hugging my chips tighter to my chest. Mrs Mitchell's eyesight might be rubbish, but her NHS specs have X-ray vision, I swear they do. It's like she's got some kind of superpower that tells her when someone's taken something that doesn't belong to them.

Her scowl deepens and I scowl back, then I turn away and roll my eyes at the new girl to show her she shouldn't give the old bat any encouragement. That's the only bit of free advice she'll get off me. She'll have to work the rest out on her own. I've got enough to do just looking after Mum.

I leave the new girl in Mrs Mitchell's clutches and run up the stairs to the third floor, the stench of chips and stolen money following me all the way.

4
Reema

I want to talk to the girl in the doorway, but I am too shy and cannot find the right words. She has bushy red hair tied in a messy knot, and her face is pale, with freckles like spots of dirt across her nose. There is an odd smell of fried food coming from her faded coat, but it is her eyes that shock me into silence.

She has the eyes of a child who has known the war.

I have seen the same look a thousand times over since the bombing began. Narrow, watchful eyes, suspicious of every new face. Hungry eyes, waiting for hours in refugee food queues. Haunted eyes, full of bad memories and troubled dreams.

This country is safe. No bombs. No war. Her blue eyes should be clear and carefree. She should not have the same eyes I see in the mirror when the nightmares wake me from my sleep.

Her eyes are all wrong.

An old lady opens the door of the apartment opposite, startling us. She is holding a box in her wrinkled hands, and she smiles at the girl and says something in English that I do not catch. I hear the words 'hello' and 'late' and 'school', and I think she is asking where the girl has been. The old lady looks friendly, but the girl is scowling. When she is asked two more 'what' questions, she starts to back towards the stairs the way a cat does when faced with a scorpion. I can almost hear her hissing.

The girl turns away, but as she does, she raises her eyes in a glance of contempt. I do not know if this is intended for me or our neighbour, but it gives me a bad feeling in the pit of my stomach. Somehow I have not made a good first impression. She does not like me. She runs up the stairs as though she wants to put a whole world of distance between us as fast as possible. I hear her footsteps reach the top floor, a key turning in a lock, and then a door slamming angrily.

I am left standing awkwardly in the hall with the old lady, who is speaking to me in rapid English and waving her box in front of my face. I give her an embarrassed smile and step back inside my apartment, hoping she will go away if I ignore her. In Aleppo before the war we had visitors all the time, but now I do not want anyone coming into our apartment in case they see Baba having a fit.

The old lady does not go away. She shuffles forward and points to the frame I am about to hang on our wall. It was a present from the women's group at the mosque I attended with Mama and Sara last Friday. I think the old lady wants to know what the Arabic words mean.

"*Ahlan wa Sahlan.*" I trace the words with my finger. "Welcome," I tell her in English.

This is the worst thing to say. The woman thinks it is an invitation. Before I can close the door she steps through the doorway and thrusts her box at me again.

"TEA!" she says loudly.

I have no choice but to invite her in now.

"I am Reema," I introduce myself hesitantly. "Please… come in. You are… welcome."

I do not mean it, but the old lady does not seem to notice.

She follows me down the narrow hallway into the cramped living room. Karen told us the family before had a boy with an even bigger wheelchair who had no problems here, but I find it hard to believe. We had to push all of the donated furniture back against the walls so that Baba does not bump his wheels against the sofa and table legs, and the kitchen is so small that he has to reverse back out if he takes something from the fridge. I can see already that he is not happy and he is trying to hide it for our sake.

Despite how disappointed I am with our new apartment, I want to be grateful so badly the effort is making me almost sick.

"Reema? Who is this?" Mama puts down the box of plates she is unpacking.

"Our next-door neighbour," I say, and then realise I know nothing else. I smile at the old lady in embarrassment. Now that Jamal, with his expensive education and fluent English, is no longer with us, I am the only one who can speak for my family in halting foreign words.

"What… is your… name?" I ask.

The old lady does not hear me. She is peering round our living room as though trying to memorise every detail. I do not know why she is so interested. We have lost everything from home – our photo albums, Jamal's science books, Sara's toys, my movie collection, Baba's tools and Mama's jewellery passed

26

down from her great-grandmother. The things in this apartment are all donated from this country, the second-hand memories of strangers that tell their stories, not ours.

I tense nervously when Baba comes in from the bedroom where he and Sara were unpacking clothes. He is already tired, and I am afraid the stress of meeting someone new will be too much for him. Sara hides behind his chair shyly when she sees the visitor, and Baba looks worried too at the sight of this strange lady in our house. He is a grown-up though, and knows how to act, even when he is nervous or embarrassed. He asks me to introduce her just like Mama did.

I try my English out again.

"What is your name?" I repeat, much louder this time. I think maybe the lady is a little deaf.

"Hmph?OhI'mMrsMitchellIlivenextdoorandIthoughtI'd bringsometeaforyourmotherandwelcomeyouintoyournewflat," she replies all in one breath. I give her another apologetic smile. I did not understand a word. She tries again.

"I-am-MRS-MITCHELL," she bellows so loud I think the girl upstairs must be able to hear her too. "Your-NEIGH-BOUR."

"Mees-us… Mee-chil?" I try, hoping I have got it right.

She nods enthusiastically and waves her tea again as though she is talking to a small child. But I am twelve, and I am neither deaf nor stupid. Her shouting is embarrassing.

Laa tankori al-ma'rouf, Reema – I hear Mama's words in my head even though she is not speaking – *Do not be ungrateful. This woman is trying.* Mama is gazing at me expectantly, and it feels for a moment as though she really is reading my mind.

"This is Mrs Mitchell from next door," I tell my family in Arabic. "She has brought tea to welcome us." Then I say in English, "This is… my mama, baba… and my… lit-tle… sis-ter Sara."

"Hello." Mrs Mitchell smiles and shakes Mama's hand. She has already grabbed Baba's hand and shaken it before I can find the words to tell her that in Syria women do not touch men they do not know. Baba sees my frown and flashes me a rare reassuring smile.

Do not worry habibti, he is saying. *This is their country, not ours. Here we must do it their way.*

It annoys me though, and I feel resentful. They call this our home, but we are not even allowed to be ourselves inside it. We are foreigners even in our own apartment.

Mama waves Mrs Mitchell into a seat and puts the kettle on while Baba tries to coax Sara out from behind his chair. Mama makes the tea that our neighbour has brought instead of using the packet of tea leaves the mosque gave us along with a big box of food supplies. She is afraid the old lady will not like our strong Syrian tea, and she wants our guest to feel welcome. I try not to make a face as I sip the weak brew. It tastes soft and sad, just like the Scottish rain. I long for a cup of strong black tea and the lashing rain of home.

"Haveyoubeenintothetownyet?" Mrs Mitchell is babbling at full speed again, and I struggle to catch anything I can translate for my family. Something about Drumhill and buses into the city. Is she saying there are lots of buses to Glasgow or hardly any?

It does not help that Sara is pulling faces at Mrs Mitchell from behind Baba's chair. The old lady says something about her sore knee, and I nearly spit my tea back into my cup, giggling when Sara mimes falling asleep with boredom. Mama frowns at me to behave even though it is Sara's fault, and I start drumming my fingers restlessly against my leg instead.

There is a printed list of prayer times from the mosque sitting on the table beside me. It is time for *Salat al-maghrib*, the evening prayer. At home, sundown comes early at the end of March in Aleppo too, but there everybody stops when the prayer call sounds from the mosques. There guests who are not Muslim understand when we stop to pray. They do not mind, and we do not have to explain.

But this woman is not from home, and she does not understand, even when I point to the prayer mats rolled up on the shelves that have our family's new Quran sitting on top in a special case. She smiles and just keeps talking. Our customs have no meaning for her, no importance.

Mama is tense and restless now too as this unwanted visitor babbles on. I do not know whether it is because she knows we are going to miss our *salat* or if she is on edge in case Baba has another seizure.

Baba can sense my concern. He throws me a warning look as I fidget, but this time I ignore him. He used to be very particular about observing prayers five times a day, but since the poison gas attack it is as though a part of his faith was damaged along with his body. Now he does not always notice when prayer times slip past. I mind though. Observing the *salat* reminds me of home, of Jamal, of all the times we were together as a family when the bombs were falling and all we had was each other and the verses from the Quran we chanted together.

I will not let this new country wash my family's traditions away in an endless trickle of weak tea and sickly rain.

I stand up and grab Sara's hand, knocking over Baba's teacup as I snatch a prayer mat from the shelf and stomp off to our bedroom. Mama calls me back, but I close the living-room door firmly behind me, marching Sara into the small bathroom so we can wash our hands before praying. Our ritual washing, *wudhu*, is supposed to help cleanse us of our thoughts and cares so that we can concentrate on God.

But no matter how hard I try, no matter how much water I splash onto my hands and over the sides of the basin, I cannot wash away the resentment I feel at the war that has driven us here.

The Fox

Twilight falls, the sunset is bleeding:
Sky-red, cloud-bandaged and weeping with rain.
The eyes of the beast-box above me are watching,
Glowing with light as the night closes in.

My belly is aching, the small ones are coming!
I swallow my whimpers and crouch in the dust.
Teeth-gritted, tail-twitching, limp-legged, clawing.
Pain-flaring, gasping… The first has arrived!

No time for comfort, the second soon follows;
Crying and mewling, makes way for a third.
Four is the loudest, blind-crawling and greedy.
But Five is the smallest: the last one, the runt.

No milk to feed them. No strength to protect them.
No den to hide from the two-legged beasts.
My body is broken, I cannot go hunting.
Soon they will weaken and then they will die.

Our bellies are empty,
We howl with the hunger.
Yes, our bellies are empty.
We *howl*.

32

5
Caylin

The newborn cubs are in danger.

Their mother's off hunting, leaving them helpless and alone. Their eyes are closed, their wee pink mouths wide open and crying for milk. They can't see the wolf creeping through the night towards them. But I can, and my fists clench tight, my stomach knotting up like a big ball of string as I watch.

There's a warning flash of amber eyes in the dark, and a huge set of jaws open right above one of the tiny cubs, hovering for one awful moment before lunging forward and snapping shut.

There's nothing I can do.

I hide my head in my hands, my own yell of horror drowning out the squeals of the cubs and the growls of the hungry hunter.

"Honestly Caylin!" Mum sighs, grabbing the remote control. "You shouldn't watch those nature programmes if you're going to get so upset over them."

She changes the channel, and we watch the end of some soppy film instead. I'd rather find out what happened to the rest of the badger cubs, but I don't complain. It doesn't matter what we watch, just as long as Mum and me are together.

I snuggle up next to her on the couch and rest my head against her fluffy dressing gown. She puts her arm round me and holds me tight as we laugh at the stupid film and the rubbish acting. This is my favourite time of day – just before bed, when Mum's slept off the doctor's tablets to help with her depression, and before she reaches for a bottle to help her through the night. This is when I can pretend we're a proper family again and the accident that ruined it all didn't ever happen.

"You want to finish those?" I reach for the plate where the last of the chips are drowning in vinegar.

"No pet, you go ahead. Thanks for getting the shopping and fixing dinner again. It's my turn tomorrow, OK? Promise."

I give Mum a fake smile as I pop a chip into my mouth and nod like I believe her. She's promised one too many times to stop wasting our benefits money on vodka and get out of bed before I come from school for me to trust her this time.

But she IS getting better, a hopeful wee voice in my head whispers. *She's got her appetite back and she even took off her pyjamas and got dressed twice this week!*

Shut up! I growl back. *I don't want to hear it!*

I can't afford to get my hopes up that Mum's finally on the mend. What if I let my guard down and someone finds out she's been staying in bed all day with a bottle of booze on the nightstand while I'm out stealing money to pay for our dinner? Social Services will have me in a children's home in a shot.

But she WAS up for you coming home today, says the wee voice that just doesn't know when to quit. *AND she washed all the minging dishes piled up by the sink. AND she finally called someone*

to come and fix the shower that's been broken for months. AND—

Shut up, SHUT UP, SHUT UP!

"Come on Caylin, time for bed." Mum interrupts my impression of a crazy person and gives my shoulder a shake to wake me up. I didn't notice I'd been nodding off and drooling down her dressing gown. "You don't want to stay up too late and be tired for school tomorrow."

I blink, wondering if I'm still half-asleep. Mum's sounding so much more like a normal mother it's starting to freak me out.

"On you go. I'll get these.' She switches off the TV and clears the plates off the coffee table while I head for the bathroom to splash water on my face. The shower's been broken for so long I can hardly remember what a proper wash actually feels like. "Don't forget to brush your teeth!" Mum calls after me.

I roll my eyes, pretending I hate being told what to do, but I smile secretly to myself while I'm sloshing a toothbrush round my mouth and trying to rinse the chip smell out of my ponytail. There's a big vinegar stain on my nightdress, but Mum's expensive vodka habit means we can't afford to buy laundry powder or the electricity to run the washing machine. We haven't done a clothes wash in ages. No wonder the other kids all laugh at me and never want to sit next to me in the dinner hall.

My bedroom's in a right guddle, with clothes piled on the floor and school books lying wherever I dropped them. I wade through a tangle of manky socks and half-finished homework exercise sheets and climb into my unmade bed, giving my pillow a suspicious sniff. It's starting to stink of Michael's

Superchippy too. I am *so* turning into one big smelly chip supper if I don't get some laundry done soon.

I'm just about to switch my lamp off when I hear Mum padding down the hall in her slippers. Instead of going straight to her own room though, she comes into mine carrying a glass of milk that she sets down on my nightstand.

"Here you go pet, in case you get thirsty. Michael went a wee bit daft with the salt and vinegar tonight, didn't he?"

I try to smile at that, but it's hard as there's a big lump in my throat. Mum used to bring me milk at bedtime every night before Grandad died. She hasn't said goodnight properly in over a year. I want to drink the glass right down there and then to show her how much I appreciate her remembering, but if I do there won't be any milk left for the cereal tomorrow. My teacher thinks I'm rubbish at maths, but I know exactly how many millilitres of milk fill half a cereal bowl and how many cartons I need to buy to get us through the week.

Mum fusses with my crumpled sheets, tutting at the big tomato soup splotches on my quilt cover as she tucks me in like she did when I was wee. Then she glances round my room, eyeing the piles of clothes and homework books like she's waking up from a bad dream and starting to see the mess for the very first time.

"I'll clean it up tomorrow," I say quickly, feeling suddenly guilty. I don't want Mum worrying about anything and reaching for the booze to calm herself down.

"No, I'll do it," Mum frowns. "It's about time this flat was put in order."

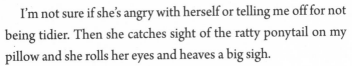

I'm not sure if she's angry with herself or telling me off for not being tidier. Then she catches sight of the ratty ponytail on my pillow and she rolls her eyes and heaves a big sigh.

"Caylin Todd! If there's one thing I've taught you, isn't it how to do your hair properly? It looks like a big bird's nest. Sit up a minute and let me fix it."

There, you see? the voice in my head says, all smug and pleased with itself like it's been proved right. *She IS getting better! When was the last time she noticed how you looked?*

I don't want to give in to the hope just yet, but I sit up and let Mum attack my hair with a brush anyway, half-enjoying the attention, half-biting my lip in pain as the tangles come out one by one. Mum's good at this. She used to be a hairdresser, but she hasn't worked in over a year. Not since Grandad died.

"You've got hair just like Gran," Mum smiles. I've heard this a billion times already, but somehow it still makes me feel good. "Mine's the same colour as hers was, but you've got the same thick curls. Just like that photo of her at Ravensholm Park, remember?"

"Yeah," I nod, trying to avoid another tug of the hairbrush that's pulling my scalp off. I don't remember the picture being taken, but I know exactly which one she's talking about. I pull a small photo album out from under my pillow and open it up, showing Mum the picture of a tall woman with a long curly ponytail. She's crouching under a tree in a park beside a chubby wee girl who's holding out her hand. They're not looking at the camera, they're both watching the squirrel that's running over to snatch a nut from the girl's outstretched palm.

"We used to go there all the time with your gran. It was her favourite place, you remember?" Mum says half to herself.

I nod again. It's another lie. Ravensholm Park's only twenty minutes away on the bus, but after Gran passed away Grandad was too sad to take me to feed the squirrels there any more. It's all just a distant blur in my head now, mixed up with Mum's second-hand stories. I wish I could remember something, *anything*, about the woman in the picture.

Mum puts the hairbrush down and turns the page of the photo album. The next picture was cut from a newspaper long before Mum was born. It's of the same woman, only much younger. She's wearing shorts and a sports vest, and she's blazing across the finish line of a race track half a metre ahead of the other runners.

"She was so fast!" Mum grins. "Just like you Caylin. You could be a runner same as her, pet. You could run for Scotland too and make us all proud."

I make a funny 'uh-mm' noise that sounds like I'm being strangled, but I don't have the guts to lie outright this time. Mum's convinced I'm going to join the school sports club this year and start winning medals just like Gran did at my age. She'd be gutted if she knew I'm too scared of failing to even try.

Mum turns the page again, and her smile suddenly fades. I glance down and totally kick myself for getting the album out to show her. Everything was going so well tonight and now I've gone and spoiled it. The next picture is of Gran and Grandad's wedding day. They're holding hands outside the church, a shower of confetti coming down like multicoloured rain.

Mum's bottom lip trembles and she shuts the album and shoves it back under my pillow. "Goodnight Caylin." Her voice sounds all tight and choked.

"Mum!" I grab her hand before she can switch the lamp off. "It wasn't your fault about Grandad. It was just an accident that he fell down the stairs and broke his hip. You couldn't have done anything!" It comes out in a rush, and I'm holding her hand so tight it's like I'm trying to hold her together, willing her not to fall apart and reach straight for the vodka again.

"I should've been there! I knew he was getting unsteady on his feet. I should've been round to see him that afternoon! I should've got to the hospital in time to say goodbye! I should've—"

Mum swallows a sob and clicks off the lamp, stumbling over my clothes in the dark and hurrying away down the hall. I hold my breath, but she doesn't go straight to her room like I want her to. Instead I can hear her shuffling about in the kitchen, switching on the light and opening the fridge. My stomach does a sick somersault when I hear the clink of a bottle being pulled out.

I TOLD you! I snarl at the smug wee voice in my head. *I told you she wasn't getting any better!*

I'd started to hope though, and the disappointment hurts worse than a million hairbrushes pulling all my tangles out at once.

"Don't forget the electrician's coming to fix the shower tomorrow!" I yell into the dark, trying to give Mum a reason to stay sober enough to get out of bed before six in the evening. "And it's your turn to fix dinner. You promised!"

Mum doesn't answer. There's a small thud, and her bedroom door closes, shutting me out.

"YOU PROMISED!" I shout again, but there's a plane flying low over the estate, and the roar of the engine drowns out my words. My voice dies to a useless whisper.

"You *promised*!"

6
Reema

I am woken by the sound of an aeroplane overhead. The engine roars above us, and I tense, barely breathing, waiting for the whine and then the ear-splitting bang as the barrel bomb explodes, sending shrapnel tearing into everything in its path.

I count to ten, slowly, silently, but there is no explosion.

Is it a dud? Or is it a chemical bomb like the one that hurt Baba?

My heart beats faster, and I see in my mind's eye the thick green gas seeping under our door, spreading through our house like fog. Chlorine gas turns to acid in your lungs. It burns you up from the inside out, choking the life out of you. Baba couldn't breathe for so long his brain was damaged, even though he was big and strong and fearless.

The gas is even more dangerous for small children.

"Sara!" I sit up in bed and reach frantically for my little sister.

And then I remember. We are not in Syria any more.

No.

We are safe, and the planes here are not carrying bombs.

I take a deep breath and let it out again, trying to push all of the fear out with it. When the sound of the plane dies away

I can hear Sara sobbing in the bed next to mine.

"Sara?" I slip out of my bed and climb in beside her. "Sara, what is wrong? Were you scared by the plane?"

"Bad dream," Sara whimpers, trying to pull the covers over her head. "The soldiers are coming with their guns."

Perhaps it is just as well the plane woke her.

I draw the covers back and put my arms around her, hugging her close until she stops shaking and her body relaxes. "There are no soldiers here, *habibti*," I whisper. "We are safe in this country. Go back to sleep."

"Is Jamal safe?" Sara asks, half-asleep. "I miss Jamal."

"I miss him too. Try not to think about it now. Go to sleep."

Sara slips back into her dreams, her fists tucked under her chin and her head lolling on my chest, but I cannot follow my own advice. I am hot and sweating; I feel as though I am a lamb stew slowly boiling in an oven. We have no photos of Jamal, and I lie awake, tossing and turning and trying to summon up an image of his face in my mind. I am so afraid of losing my memories of him, there are tears running down my cheeks by the time I remember exactly what my big brother looked like.

When I close my eyes it is not a picture of his face when I last saw him nearly nine months ago that fills my head. It is a memory of how he used to look before the war that comes back to me, and it makes me smile to myself in the dark.

Yes. There he is, with the mop of messy black hair that grew so fast I would tease him for looking like a girl until he went to the barber to get it chopped short again. I can also remember the short fuzz on his chin that he was so proud of. I can see his eyes staring back at me clearly now, full of laughter, even though he was the most dedicated student at his school. Jamal was going to be a doctor. When the war began and he could not start university, he volunteered at the hospital helping the sick and wounded. Good experience, he called the hard work. He always saw the bright side of everything.

His voice is speaking in my head. I can hear him so clearly he could be standing next to me at the school gate where he met me every day and took me home.

"Race you, Little Gazelle. Let us see who reaches the market first."

I look up at him, twice my height and three times as broad, and know today is the day I will beat him without him letting me win.

"You are too old and slow!" I shout, already running down the street. "You could not catch me if you tried!"

I hear Jamal laugh behind me and the sound of his shoes hitting the ground as he runs to catch up. But he will not catch me today. I race past the basketball court in the school yard and across the road, dodging the slow-moving traffic snarled up in the narrow street and ignoring the shouts of drivers who are tired and grumpy in the late afternoon heat. The bright yellow of the taxis blends with the orange of the minibuses until it looks like the sun is setting right here in the road.

The sky above is still blue though. An endless vivid blue that makes my heart sing to look up at it.

"Reema, wait!" Jamal calls behind me. He is already out of

breath, and I smile to myself and keep running. He has his brains and his books and my parents' dreams of a successful career, but I have one thing my perfect big brother does not have.

I have fast legs.

The ladies coming out of the beauty parlour with their hair piled up in curls ready for the weekend scold me when I brush too close to their long skirts, and I stick my tongue out at the shoe-shine boys sitting outside the hotel café who hoot and cheer as I race past.

Jamal often takes me for ice cream after school, but not today. Today is special. Today is my birthday, and Jamal has promised to buy me something from the *souks*, the markets that crowd the streets all the way to the Citadel on the hill.

I slow as I reach the meat *souks*, with their beef and mutton hanging on hooks and the vendors battling with flies in the afternoon heat. I am not tired, not yet. But the *souks* are even busier than usual on a Thursday, crowded with shoppers stocking up for the weekend that starts tomorrow, and for the meal they will prepare for their family after Friday prayers in the mosque. I stop by the row of shoe menders, listening to the hum of their sewing machines and waiting for Jamal to catch up. I am only nine, and I do not want to get lost in the crowd.

"I beat you today!" I grin up at him when he jogs to a halt and catches hold of my hand. "I can outrun ANYBODY!"

"So you can, Little Gazelle, so you can." Jamal is panting and gripping my hand tightly as though he is afraid I will run off again and disappear in the crowd. There is a new look in his eyes, one that I have not seen before. My heart swells with

pride; my big brother's respect is the best birthday present he could ever give me.

But there is one more gift to come, and we head down the main street of Souk al-Attarin. The covered markets are a labyrinth of colour and noise and smells, and so many people I wonder if the whole of Aleppo has a birthday to celebrate today. Narrow lanes branch off from the main thoroughfare, full of stalls selling everything from woven carpets and copper teapots to hubble-bubble water pipes and chess sets.

We are heading for the jewellery section, further up off Souk az-Zarb, when I stop. Something at one of the textile stalls has caught my eye. Something so breezy and light it would float off on the wind if it were not tied to the display stand by a loose knot. It is a headscarf, like the ones Mama wears, but more beautiful than any I have ever seen.

It is green like the sea when the wind catches the waves, and the scarf's silk strands shimmer like sunlight on water. I pull on Jamal's hand and point, my voice eager above the noise of the crowd.

"That one Jamal! That is what I want for my birthday."

"A headscarf?" Jamal fingers the soft fabric and throws me a puzzled look. "It is pretty Reema, but would you not prefer a necklace or a bracelet?"

"No, that is what I want. I am sure, Jamal, I am sure!"

"But you are far too young to cover your head, that is for older girls and women. You have such beautiful hair, Reema, what do you want to hide it for?" He gives my long, thick braid a playful tug, and starts to walk away.

"Please Jamal, please! That is what I want for my birthday, nothing else."

I do not know why, but I am almost crying now. All I know is that the sea and the sunlight are woven into that scarf, and I want it so badly I am prepared to beg my brother on my knees if I have to.

I do not have to. Jamal sees the tears in my eyes and turns back. "Do not cry *habibti*. If you want it so badly, of course you can have it for your birthday."

He talks to the vendor while I bounce on my toes in excitement, my fingers tingling with anticipation until a price is agreed and the scarf is handed over. Jamal helps me cover my head and wind the long ends around my neck, and I feel like I am wrapped in the cool breath of the sea. I look up at the patch of blue sky beyond the row of stalls, and feel as though every ray of sunshine in the whole of Syria is being soaked up by my special shimmering scarf.

And then the world goes dark.

My eyes are still open, but I cannot see anything until the choking grey dust settles. When the world emerges from the swirling ash everything is different. The stalls have shut down and the *souks* are rubble. Somewhere out of sight I can hear the sound of people sobbing. This is no longer my memory. This is a bad dream.

The patch of sky is no longer blue, but heavy with cloud and humming a deep warning note. An aircraft is coming, flying too low above the silent streets. There is a knot of fear and dread in the pit of my stomach that tightens as the engine roar draws nearer.

"Jamal, we must run!" I cry.

And that is when I realise Jamal is no longer holding my hand.

He is gone.

All that remains is the scream of the engine and the whistle of a barrel bomb falling on the street before me.

"JAMAL!"

7
Caylin

I sit up in bed with a start. A loud cry in the night shook me awake, and I hold my breath, listening. I don't think it came from Mum's room. I think it came from outside.

I scramble over to the window and peer out into the night. In the moonlight the Drumhill estate is silent, the quiet only disturbed every few minutes by the planes that roar overhead to Glasgow airport. When my eyes are used to the dark I can see all the way to the row of houses that circle the swing park. My brain's still a bit sleep-muddled, and before I know what I'm doing I'm counting five houses along from the left and checking to see if Grandad's got his kitchen light on to keep away the burglars. Then suddenly I'm wide awake, and my stomach cramps tight when I remember that Grandad is gone.

I tear my eyes away from his old house and look down at the wee strip of ground behind our flats, trying to find what's making the strange howling noise. The Council calls it a garden, but it's just a muddy dumping ground full of weeds and scrawny bushes that has a path leading up to the bin shed by the back wall. Mrs Mitchell's always on at the Council about

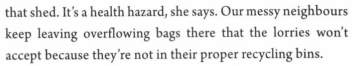

that shed. It's a health hazard, she says. Our messy neighbours keep leaving overflowing bags there that the lorries won't accept because they're not in their proper recycling bins.

I hear the cry again, and I peer into the dark alley that runs between our back wall and the gardens of the flats opposite. It's not coming from there though, the noise is closer than that.

It's coming from our bin shed.

I don't know what it is that makes me grab my jacket and go down to take a look.

Maybe there's a dog out there that's been hurt, or maybe it's a little kid who's gone missing like the one I saw on the news tonight, and I can be a hero by finding him first.

I hurry down the stairs, my slippers silent on the concrete steps. When I reach the bottom I stop, making sure there's no sound of movement from Mrs Mitchell's flat. There's no door on either end of the passageway, and the wind blows right through from front to back. I slip out into the garden, shivering in the cold and trying to pretend I'm braver than I feel.

It's all quiet for a minute, and then another plane passes so low on its way to the airport I'm half-scared it'll take our roof off.

When the engine roar finally fades away in the distance I hear something else.

Shuffling.

Snuffling.

A funny kind of whining.

It's coming from the bin shed, but when I go to look there's nothing there but smelly black bags. I check behind them. Nothing.

49

The noises have gone quiet, like something's heard me and is holding its breath.

That's when I think to look behind the shed.

I nearly jump out of my skin when I see yellow eyes staring back at me.

It's a fox, and she growls at me so fierce and low that at first I want to run straight back up to my room. I was bitten on the leg in the park by a dog when I was wee, and I can still remember how much it hurt. Grandad had to take me to the hospital to get the bite cleaned and have doctors stick me full of needles. That was a pet dog though. This is a wild animal.

I'm about to leave her be when I see there's something wrong with her. I look closer. She's not sitting up, but lying on her side, panting. Her growl is angry, but her eyes are afraid. She has a red coat and a dirty white belly with a big dark patch that's heaving up and down. It looks like she's struggling for breath, but when I take another step towards her I can see the dark patch is actually a huddle of tiny cubs all sucking hard for milk. The fox looks too skinny to be able to feed them.

I stare at them, a warm feeling of wonder filling up the dark places in my stomach that are usually big holes of worry and hunger and guilt. The fox is trying to get up and move away, but her front leg is bleeding and won't hold her weight. I can see now the spots of darker red on her coat are dried blood, and there are a couple of deep gashes down her side that are still bleeding. She looks like she's been hit by a car. The blind cubs are all shaken loose when she moves and start whimpering for milk. It makes me feel so sad I want to cry.

Feeling brave, I pull off my jacket and tuck it round them, trying to avoid the snapping jaws of the fox who wants to take my hand off. She looks as hungry as I do at the end of the week when the benefits money runs out. I didn't buy anything at the shops today that I can give them, just toilet roll and toothpaste and tins of beans and soup for Mum to eat while I'm at school. But tomorrow's Friday, when Mum'll have her money for the next week paid straight into her account. I know her number, so I'll nip down to the cash machine by Michael's Superchippy and get out enough to buy food for the foxes and pay the electricity bill.

If Mum wants to make a fuss about it she can drag herself out of bed for once and stop me.

Huh, like that's ever going to happen.

I'll have food for the foxes tomorrow. Tonight they'll have to make do with my old jacket. I have another one anyway, the one Mum got me at Christmas. She wasn't sober when she bought it and it's too big, but at least it doesn't smell of greasy chips like this one does.

The fox is too tired to do more than snarl at me feebly, but when she sees I haven't taken her cubs and feels the warmth from my jacket, she stops growling and just stares back at me with those big yellow eyes.

"I'm Caylin," I tell her, "and I'm going to look after you."

The warm feeling spreads when I say this until my whole body's tingling with happiness. "I'll keep you safe, you and your cubs. I'll keep you warm and fed, I'll keep you hidden. I'll keep you secret – I'm good at secrets."

This fox is my responsibility. A secret that doesn't make me sick to my stomach for once.

My best secret.

Mine.

8

Reema

The loud cry in the night gives me such a fright I nearly drop my glass of water in the sink.

What was that?

I shiver in the dark kitchen, gritting my teeth until the roar of another passenger jet flying overhead dies away. Baba has not slept well since the chemical attack and I hope the noises do not disturb him. I wait, but I do not hear the strange cry again.

Perhaps I was imagining it. Perhaps it was just the aeroplane engine.

I tiptoe back through the living room, silently cursing the people who put us in an apartment so close to an airport when every memory we have is haunted by screaming aircraft engines and the fear of falling bombs.

Before I can reach my room though, a long howl wails through the corridor outside. I hurry up the narrow hall and press my ear to the front door, listening carefully. I think I hear footsteps dying away on the stairs.

I heard footsteps in the streets of Aleppo at night too. When the war began soldiers came banging on doors in the dark. I was so scared they would take Baba and Jamal away, there were some nights I would pray non-stop until the sun came up.

I should go back to bed…

Instead I take my coat from the rack on the wall and pull it over my nightdress. Then I open the door carefully and peer into the dark corridor beyond. There is only silence now.

And then another sound.

It is the bark of a dog, or perhaps a bigger, wilder animal.

I really should go back to bed…

I tiptoe out into the corridor, following the cold breeze to the back entrance that leads to a little wilderness beyond. I think once it was a garden, but now it is overgrown with bushes and weeds, and there are plastic boxes and broken bicycle wheels and polystyrene packaging slabs lying scattered in the mud.

A soft growling whine is coming from the shelter full of trash cans at the bottom of the garden. I step onto the path and tiptoe closer.

This is foolish. I do not know whether there are wolves and jackals in this strange country. I should not explore any further.

It is time to go back to bed…

I tilt my head and listen again, hearing snuffling and whining and soft, low whimpers coming from behind the shelter. I pick up a heavy stick and peer into the space between the back of the shelter and the garden's stone wall. What I see there makes me drop the stick in surprise.

It is a family of foxes, all wrapped up in a smelly old coat the mother fox must have pulled from the trash. She blinks at me in the moonlight, wary and warning, but I can see she is injured and in no state to care for the cubs that are sucking desperately for milk.

She is hungry. They all are.

I turn and run back up the path, leaving the front door of our apartment wide open in my haste to get to the kitchen.

What do foxes eat? I wonder, rummaging around in the fridge and trying to read the unfamiliar labels on the tins of donated food. *I wish Jamal was here. He would know.*

I remember the time Jamal rescued a bag full of puppies from the Queiq River where someone had thrown them away to drown. Baba would not have them in the house. He said they would make us unclean and we would have to wash our clothes before prayers if we touched them. But for months Jamal paid his lunch money to the man who ran the bicycle repair shop near our apartment, to let him keep them in the back room. He fed them every day with milk and eggs, and then scraps from the smaller stalls at the meat *souk*. When the puppies were big enough he went round our Christian neighbours asking if they would like a dog for free. He found homes for them all. Baba always knew when Jamal had been with the dogs, as he washed his clothes himself instead of putting them in the laundry basket. But he didn't tell Jamal off, because the Quran teaches that we must be kind to animals.

I do not think Baba would like me feeding foxes like pet dogs though.

"Do not let Mama see you bringing food to the foxes either, my silly *ukhti assaghira*!" I can hear Jamal laughing at me in my head. "Or she will scream in horror and lock you in the closet to stop you going anywhere near wild animals with rabies and scabies and plague ever again!"

I can still hear his warm laugh echoing in my head as I stand in our cold kitchen, spooning the remains of rice and meat from our evening meal into a plastic bowl. I do not know if this is what foxes eat, I only know that feeding them is what Jamal would have done. I will do anything to keep his voice in my head alive, even if it risks making Mama and Baba angry with me if they ever find out.

I fill a smaller bowl with milk and eggs and carry them carefully out to the back garden. The fox growls when she sees I have returned, but as soon as she smells the food she tries to sit up, her ears alert. Her leg will not support her though, so I place the bowls next to her, careful not to touch her fur and make myself unclean. She sniffs at the contents suspiciously, looking up at me with wary yellow eyes.

I take a step back, showing her I mean no harm.

At once she eats ravenously, slurping the milk and slopping it over the sides of the bowl before attacking the meat and rice. It is clear she has not eaten in days.

"I am Reema," I tell the fox, "and I will not let you and your cubs go hungry."

The fox stops eating for a long moment and stares at me. I do not know if she understands, but the suspicion has gone from her eyes.

"You need a name," I say. But what she really needs is the freedom to run wild again and look after her young by herself. A name is all I have to offer her tonight.

"I will call you *Hurriyah*," I say softly to the fox in Arabic, and then in halting English I add, "I will… call you… *Freedom*."

I do not know why I have chosen this word out of all the many more suitable ones I could have picked. I only know that it is her name. And it is also a wish for her future.

I smile in the darkness as I gaze at Hurriyah and her cubs cuddled up in the old coat.

For the first time in this strange land I have something I can call my own, something to care about and hope for.

Something called Freedom.

9
Caylin

I haven't been so excited to get out of bed for ages. There's a My Little Pony digital alarm clock on my nightstand, and it's showing ten past seven. It's too young for me now, that clock, but it was a Christmas present from my grandad when I was wee and I'd eat my own hand rather than throw it away. The first number doesn't light up any more, but if I chucked out everything round here that doesn't work properly then every single thing we own would end up in the bin shed. Me and Mum included.

After I pull on the unwashed uniform I've been wearing all week, I coax my hair into a messy ponytail and go to check on Mum, slipping her bank card out of her handbag. I'm expecting her to be out cold, an empty bottle of vodka on her nightstand and a pile of snot-stained tissues piled round the bed from crying herself to sleep. But that's not what I find.

The bottle's sitting right where I expect it to be, but it's still full. She hasn't touched the vodka. She kept her promise after all.

I'm grinning so hard my face hurts as I tiptoe into the kitchen and put the bottle back in the fridge so it's out of reach. I make her a quick cup of tea to sit on her nightstand instead, in case she wakes up while I'm out. After I've gone to the cash machine I'll go to the store and get bread and peanut butter so I can leave her sandwiches before school too. I'd do anything to make it easier for her to get out of bed and back on her feet. It's all I've cared about for months.

But it's not the thought of feeding Mum that has me running down the road at quarter to eight, long before the other kids from my school are up and about. I have something new to think about today, something that has me almost hugging myself in excitement.

I have a family of foxes to look after.

I almost don't care that when I've been to the cash machine and jogged down to the early opening Spar there's a group of teenagers hanging round outside smoking.

Almost.

A couple of the girls nudge each other and snigger as I hurry past, but I keep my head down and run at the automatic doors so fast they barely have time to open for me. Today I'm a secret agent on a mission – codename: Breakfast – and even the enemy isn't going to stop me feeding my foxes before school.

Luckily, the checkout woman with suspicious eyes isn't at work yet and there's only a spotty guy who looks like he's playing on his mobile phone behind the counter.

Even better.

I check the position of the security cameras and swipe a packet of chocolate biscuits as I pass the snack aisle, shoving them in my pocket and moving on quickly to the tinned goods. These are harder to pinch. I usually have to pay for them.

I've taken more from Mum's bank account than I usually do, but I still check each of the prices carefully, adding them up in my head and working out exactly what I'll need to get us through the week and have some left over for the foxes too. I may be rubbish at Mrs Gibb's fractions and decimals, but I'm a pro when it comes to the shopping bill.

Even with a basket full of out-of-date Irish stew and meatballs that have been marked down less than half-price, there's not going to be enough food for all of us. Unless someone else at school has birthday cash or a fistful of pocket money for me to swipe, I'll have to find another way to fill the cupboards.

I glance at the row of corned beef tins and pink Spam.

I bet the fox would love them.

There's a deep pocket inside my stupidly big Christmas jacket, and I pull my zip down slowly, trying to look innocent, like I'm just too hot. My hand hovers over a tin, and I check the security cameras again, turning slightly so my back is to the nearest one.

The tin's off the shelf and halfway inside my pocket before I realise I'm being watched.

The new girl with the headscarf from the flat downstairs is standing at the corner of the aisle, looking at me with big brown disapproving eyes. I shove the tin down into my pocket and pull my zip up quickly, trying to pretend I wasn't doing anything dodgy. The girl's eyes are like searchlights though, and I can feel myself shrinking into a ball of shame as she turns to whisper something to her wee sister and the tall woman standing beside them.

I don't know if they're talking about me or not, but I put my head down and run for the bread aisle like I'm being chased by a swarm of bees.

By the time my cheeks have stopped burning and I've put the last of the messages I'm willing to pay for into my basket, I'm pretty sure the girls and their mother will be long gone and the coast will be clear.

That's why I get such a nasty shock when I head to the till and find them standing right in front of me.

The tall woman with the blue headscarf looks like she's tipped the entire contents of her purse over the counter. She's counting coins out slowly, looking to the guy at the till for help. He's not bothering though, he's just fiddling with his phone with a bored look on his face, waiting for her to sort it out herself.

"Get a move on," the guy behind me mutters loud enough for the whole queue to hear. The woman doesn't understand, but she knows what the loud sighs and eye-rolls from the people waiting impatiently behind her mean.

The girl with the green headscarf tries to help with the coins, but she clearly hasn't understood how much the checkout guy asked for. Her wee sister with long black plaits looks so nervous I think she's going to cry. They're both wearing the same school uniform as me. Maybe that's what makes me shuffle up to the counter to help them out.

"How much?" I ask, taking the pile of coins from the girl and counting the money out quickly. She looks at me suspiciously, like she's not sure if I'm going to steal it or not, but her mother smiles at me gratefully, so I ignore headscarf-girl and hand the money to the plook-faced troll playing on his phone.

When they've packed their shopping away and I'm getting my own stuff scanned, the tall woman says something in a funny language to the older girl, who takes a deep breath and says, "Sankyew. I… am… Reema. You… walk to… school… with us."

I'm not sure if it's a question or a command. Either way I have to say no. I have foxes to feed and sandwiches to make for Mum first.

"Not today. I've got things to do before school."

The girl frowns, fumbling for my meaning.

"No." I shake my head to make it clearer. "Can't. Sorry."

The girl's hopeful smile fades, and it's like a light's gone out behind her bright brown eyes. She's probably scared stiff starting a new school in a different country where she can't understand a word anyone's saying. I don't know what that's like, but I do know how it feels to be alone at school with no one to talk to.

I try not to feel bad as they walk away. I've got enough to do feeding Mum and the foxes. I can't look after everyone.

After I've paid I heave the bulging backpack over my shoulders and head for the door, my box of washing powder and loaf of bread cradled in my arms so they won't get crushed. When I get back outside the girls and their mother are gone, but the high-school kids are still there. I think they've been waiting.

"Hey Caylin, you want a smoke?"

One of the girls pulls her cigarette from her mouth and tries to stub it out on my neck as I shuffle past. The other fourth-years laugh, and a couple more cigarette butts are flicked my way and bounce off my new Christmas jacket. I shrink lower beneath the weight of my backpack and walk faster.

"Come back you wee skank, we're talking to you!"

One of the boys steps forward and tries to grab hold of my hood.

I'm not stupid. I'll be starting high school this autumn, and I know when the fourth-years push me around I'm going to have to stand up for myself, even if it means getting leathered.

But not today.

Today I do the one thing that can still get me out of trouble.

Today I run.

The tins in my bag bang against my back as I take off down the road, and I feel so slow it's like I'm wading through the porridge Grandad used to make. It's fast enough that the fourth-years with their lungs full of smoke don't want to follow though. I'm not worth it. They have more important things to care about than me.

Mrs Mitchell's just leaving for her morning coffee club when I get back, but I run past before she can ask where I've been. She'll be too busy at the community centre gossiping about the new family to pay any attention to me today either. I should be able to slip out and feed the foxes in peace.

When I'm arranging the tins in the kitchen I get another shock. Mum comes shuffling down the hall in her nightgown, holding the mug I left her.

"Thanks for the tea, pet. It was just what I needed."

I stand gawping at her in amazement. "What are you doing up at this time?"

"The electrician's coming to fix the shower, remember?" Mum yawns. "Some guy Trish at the doctor's recommended.

63

Oh! Did you get the shopping? You didn't need to do that, I said I'd sort it today. "

"It's no problem," I say quickly, hoping Mum hasn't noticed the extra cans of meatballs and stew I've stashed behind the empty biscuit tin.

"I should get dressed, shouldn't I? Can't open the front door to some stranger in this." Mum points at her leopard-print dressing gown and fluffy pink slippers. I grin back at her, so happy she's finally noticed it's not right to spend all day in her pyjamas that I could burst.

"See you after school, pet," Mum says, and the smile's wiped from my face when she gives me a hug and the packet of stolen biscuits and tin of corned beef in my pocket dig into us both. Mum frowns, and for a minute I'm worried she's going to ask what I'm hiding in my coat, but it's my manky school uniform she's looking at.

"God Caylin, when was the last time your clothes were washed?" She gives my sweatshirt a sniff and wrinkles up her nose.

"Umm… sorry, I'll put them in the machine this weekend. I got washing powder, see?" I point to the box I've lugged all the way back from the shops.

"It's not your job, pet." Mum smoothes my collar down sadly. Her bottom lip's quivering again, but I'm not sure what's upset her this time until she says, "I've been a rubbish mum this year, haven't I?"

"You've been sad. It's not your fault." I don't know if it's the right thing to say, but since she gives me a watery smile and heads back to her room with a fresh cup of tea instead of the bottle of vodka, I think it might be.

I glance at the clock and swear under my breath. I'll need to be quick if I want to feed the foxes and get to school on time. I open the tin of corned beef and mash it into a bowl, then I sneak out the door and run down the stairs two at a time.

The fox is awake behind the bin shed, but the cubs are all asleep, still curled up on her belly with my jacket round them. I wonder if the fox has had any sleep since her babies arrived. Her yellow eyes watch me suspiciously, but I can't tell if she's tired.

All I know is she looks hungry.

She doesn't growl at me this time, and when I set the bowl down next to her she starts eating without even sniffing it first. I smile and put my hand out to pat her, but as soon as I move her head jerks up and she snaps at me, her jaws almost taking my fingers off.

"Sorry, you're not a dog, I forgot." I stick my hand back in my pocket so she can see I'm not going to touch her again. Not yet anyway. Not till she trusts me.

Her cubs wake up when she finishes the food and start sucking away again like tiny wee milk vampires. Their downy fur is dark and their pink bellies fill like balloons until I'm scared they're going to pop. When they're done they snuggle back into their mother's fur, sleepy and satisfied. I want to sit here and watch them all day, but I have to get to school.

"I'll be back tonight with more food," I tell the fox, hiding the bowl away behind a bush. I don't want Mrs Mitchell seeing it.

She'd have Pest Control on the fox and her cubs for sure if she found out they were here.

"Go to sleep Poppy, you'll be safe till then."

Poppy.

I didn't even know that's what I was going to call her until I said it. It must be her fur. It reminds me of the orangey-red of the flowers I found down by the sand dunes the very last time I went to the beach with Grandad. It's one of the happiest memories I have, and even the worry over Mum and how she couldn't cope after he died can't erase it.

Poppy and her cubs make me happy too.

I take one last look behind the bin shed to say goodbye to them, then I sling my backpack over my shoulder and head to school, running down the road like my feet are dancing on sunshine.

10
Reema

I have felt sick all morning. The first day at my new school seems to have lasted a thousand years, and it is still only lunchtime.

"Hurry up!" The boy behind me in the canteen queue gives me an impatient shove, and I shuffle forward, blinking at the rows of strange food on the counter and wondering if the meat in the sandwiches is *halal*. Probably not. I settle on a thin slice of greasy-looking pizza and a small plate of chips as the safest choice. They are the only things I recognise. Even the smells coming from the kitchen are hard to identify.

"Move it, cloth ears."

A group of girls from my class barge past with their loaded trays as I stand hesitating by the service hatch. I start to follow them to their table, but a girl called Lisa puts her hand over the empty seat beside her so I cannot sit down.

"It's for Zoe," she snaps.

I do not understand until a girl from the year below us slips into the seat and frowns at me when she sees I am still hovering. There are no more empty seats at the table, and I do not know where to sit. Fatima from the Refugee Council met us at the school gate this morning to take us to the head teacher and translate for us. After we were shown our classes though and Mama and Fatima left, I was on my own. My teacher is not like Sara's. My little sister's teacher is sitting next to her and eating lunch with the primary two class, smiling at Sara and helping her to make friends with the other children. Mrs Gibb said she would show me the lunch hall too, but when the bell rang she left class with her empty coffee mug and did not return.

I do not want to embarrass my sister and myself by sitting with the infant classes. I must manage this alone.

"Watch it, cloth ears," I hear again when I nearly trip over the feet of a boy who is sitting with his legs sprawled out in the aisle. *Cloth ears.* I have heard other children use the phrase many times today and I am only just starting to understand that they are making fun of my headscarf.

I swallow the hurt down and head for the table at the far side of the canteen. I see the children here all have free school lunch trays like me instead of packed lunches and this is where the other asylum seekers at the school are sitting. There are two younger girls from the Congo who I met in the playground at break, but they have been here for several years and have made friends already. There is no room left to sit beside them. I keep moving.

Then I hear something that makes my heart dance.

"...*qallam... kitaab...*"

The Arabic words for pen and book. Someone is speaking my language!

I hurry down the row to where a group of three girls and two boys from the middle grades are leaning over their homework books and comparing notes as they eat. They have dark hair and eyes just like me, and they do not even glance at my headscarf when I sit down next to them and give them my warmest smile. I long so much to speak to someone from home I am almost shaking.

"*Salaam Aleykum*," I say, loud enough to make them look up from their books again.

"*Salaam*," they nod politely, then go straight back to talking to each other.

My smile fades as I listen. I do not recognise most of their words; they are almost as difficult to understand as English. I was mistaken. They are not speaking Arabic after all. They are from Pakistan and they are speaking Urdu.

I sit staring at the pizza and chips going cold on my tray, unable to eat. My stomach is too full of disappointment and loneliness for me to feel hungry now. I glance at the clock on the wall and that makes me feel even worse. The midday prayer time is slipping past and I have nowhere quiet to go for *salat*. Sara and I could not go back to our apartment for lunch today as Baba is going to the hospital to start physiotherapy for his nerve damage. I nearly cried when Mama told me she and Fatima were going with him, and Sara and I would have to stay in school for lunch.

I remember my harsh words to her this morning and they make me feel so ashamed I want to hide under the canteen table to escape them.

"But Mama," I wailed, "why do we have to start school today? Why can it not wait until Monday? It is already our Syrian weekend."

Mama sighed, the way she always does when she is angry or upset. "I told you Reema, Friday is a working day in this country, not a holiday. We will all have to get used to that."

It is not right. Friday is our special day, the middle of our weekend. I should be going to the mosque with my family, not going to school.

Everything here is all wrong.

"It is not fair!" I yelled. "I hate it here. When can we go home, Mama? When will the war be over?" I realised that I sounded like Sara instead of a twelve year old, and that made me even angrier.

Mama saw my lip trembling, and her face softened. "You can pray when you come home after school, Reema. Allah will not mind if you are a little late. And we will go to the mosque this evening, *inshallah*." Mama always finishes her sentences about the future with 'God willing' and I know I should too, though I often forget.

"All of us?" I asked hopefully. "Baba too?"

"We will see."

Inshallah, I repeat to myself now as I play with my cold chips. *Inshallah*.

I want Baba to get well and for us all to go to the mosque together as a family so much it hurts. I know I should be grateful for this foreign food though, and force myself to eat it instead of toying with it. I know what it feels like to be hungry, and I know there are many people back home in Syria and in the refugee camps who would be thankful for this one small plate of chips and slice of greasy pizza.

They are not the only ones who are desperate for food.

70

I remember my fox, whimpering with hunger behind the shelter in the garden. I did not have time to feed Hurriyah this morning. I could not slip out secretly before school, we were too busy putting on our new uniforms and making breakfast and shopping. The thought of her waiting for me, her belly growling painfully and her cubs crying for milk makes my heart ache so hard I can barely breathe.

I only realise I am crying when a grubby piece of toilet roll is thrust under my nose. I look up. The girl from my apartment building is slouched at the table across from me, holding out a tissue that looks like it has been used several times already.

I take it anyway and wipe my nose gratefully. It smells even more like chips than the cold ones on my plate, but I do not mind. Someone has taken notice of me at last.

"Thank... you... Cay-lin." I know the girl's name now. Our teacher has been shouting it all morning. I do not think Caylin is a good student. I do not think she is a good person either. I saw her stealing from the shop before school, and when the boy sitting beside her in class used her pen without asking she kicked him so hard under the table he nearly cried. She has not talked to me at all today, even though the teacher gave me the seat opposite her. She does not look friendly, but I have no one else to talk to, and I have to try.

"I... am Reema," I tell her again, unsure if she remembers my name.

"Duh." Caylin rolls her eyes, and I catch her meaning even though I do not understand the word. I try to return her tissue, but she makes another face and goes back to cramming chips

71

into her mouth so quickly I am worried she will choke. She looks as hungry as the fox. I have seen that look before many times back home, but I was not expecting to see it here where there is plenty of food.

"You... like?" I offer her my plate of chips. They are cold now, but after only a quick glance at me to make sure I am serious Caylin takes the plate and wolfs them down as though she has not eaten in a long time. When she is finished she wipes her hands on her shabby uniform, then shifts awkwardly in her seat as though she is trying to think of something to say to me. She does not say thank you. Instead she hunts around in her pocket until she finds a small packet and holds it out to me across the table.

"Chewths?" she asks.

"Choose?" I blink. Is she asking me to select one of the small sticks inside? They all look the same to me. They are all squashed flat like they have been living in Caylin's pocket for years.

"Chewing gum," Caylin says more slowly.

"Ah! Chew-ing gum!" I smile, finally recognising the word. I do not take a stick though. I am sure Caylin has stolen this packet from the shop too.

"Yeah, that's right," Caylin nods, her face brightening when she sees she has been understood. "Look. Fork." She holds up the piece of cutlery she has not bothered using.

"Fork," I repeat. I know this word already, but I want to encourage Caylin to keep talking to me. "This?" I ask, pointing to the plate sitting on my tray.

"Plate," Caylin says, slowly enough for me to catch.

"Pleat?" I try.

"Play–Tih," Caylin repeats. She is a better teacher than Mrs Gibb, who talks far too fast for me to understand.

"Plate," I say again, and Caylin grins at me as though she has helped me do something clever. She has a nice smile. I have only ever seen her scowling until now. I did not know she even knew how to smile. "This one?" I point to the last chip left on my plate. I know what it is called, but I want to get the Scottish accent just right so I do not sound so foreign.

"Chipths," Caylin says, a little reluctantly.

"Chip-ths?" I copy. Caylin's smile disappears. I do not know if I have got the accent wrong, but Caylin's frown puts me off trying to say it again. "And this?" I point to the slice of cold pizza on my plate.

Caylin looks even more reluctant, glancing round to make sure no one else is listening.

"Pitha," she says at last, too low for me to catch.

"Sor-ry?"

"Pi-THA," she repeats louder.

"Ah. PEE-THA," I copy.

"PEETHA AND CHIPTHS!" I hear a group of children from our class giggling as they walk past with their empty trays. I am sure they are laughing at my accent, but it is Caylin who turns bright red.

"Peetha and chipths … ?" I ask, pointing to the food and trying to make sure I have the accent right this time.

Caylin slams her hand down on the table so hard our plates shake.

"THOP IT!" she hisses, her whole face twisting up in fury. "Thay it again and I'll kill you, understhdand?"

I do understand. Her words are slow and clear despite the strange hissing sound her tongue makes. I understand the dangerous glint in her eyes and the look of disgust she throws me as she jumps up and marches away.

The only thing I do not understand is what I have done wrong.

11
Caylin

When home time finally comes I can't get out fast enough. I want to get a hundred miles away from Mrs Gibb and her stupid lessons, and a million miles away from that new girl who copies my lisp and makes people laugh at me.

I want to get back to Poppy and her cubs.

I was so busy thinking about them all day that I didn't even mind not having anyone to play with at break. I saw Zoe from 6B whispering to Lisa from my class all the way through lunch, and when we got outside there was a big group of girls sitting at one of the picnic tables staring at me. I know they were talking about me stealing Zoe's birthday money, but none of them had the guts to come over and challenge me about it.

I'd better be careful though. Lisa's the most popular girl in school, and her big sister's one of the fourth-years who hang around the shops and have a go at me whenever I walk past. If Zoe's friends with Lisa now, I'd better not try and take any more money off her.

She's not the one I want to thump today anyway. After the way Reema embarrassed me, it's her I'd like to flatten.

I thought she'd be a total scoosh to beat in a fight when I first saw her, but now I'm not so sure. She's all strung out and skinny like a piece of gum that's been chewed too hard, but there's a tough look in her eyes that I don't like. Something tells me she wouldn't be a pushover like the other girls in my class.

If she makes fun of my lisp one more time I'll take her on though, tough or not, I promise myself as I run down the road.

In less than five minutes I'm back at the flats, clattering up the ramp and bounding up the stairs three at a time.

As soon as I put my key in the lock I know that something's different.

The door's already unlocked and swings open under my hand. That means Mum's been out of the house today, and not for vodka, as there's still a full bottle sitting in the fridge. There's the sound of music playing on the radio and I can hear Mum laughing in the kitchen. I'm so happy she's out of bed and waiting for me to come home from school like she used to that I dance along with the music all the way to the kitchen.

Maybe she's making me toast and jam and we can sit and watch TV and I can tell her all about my day and everything will finally be back to normal! I think all in a rush. We haven't got any jam, but that doesn't stop me fantasising. We're going to be a proper family again and nothing's going to spoil that for me now.

I stop dancing when I reach the kitchen door, the big bubble of happiness in my chest fizzing away to nothing when I see what's going on inside. Mum isn't waiting for me to come home after all. She's having a cup of tea with the shower repairman and they're eating the biscuits I pinched this morning. Those were for my lunch tomorrow. That's the only treat I get, watching cartoons on a Saturday like I used to at Grandad's house and eating half a pack of chocolate biscuits. I can only have a couple a day after that to make them last the whole week, but the two of them have finished most of the packet between them. It makes me so mad I want to smash the empty biscuit tin over the repairman's head.

"Oh, there you are Caylin." Mum smiles at me like she's always there waiting for me to come home from school instead of being out cold in bed. "Come and meet Brian. He's fixed our shower and he's even sorted out the faulty plug on the kettle."

"Hi Caylin, how was school?"

Brian smiles at me too and I frown back at him to show just how unwelcome he is. I don't care how many plugs he fixes in our flat, he still has no right to my chocolate biscuits.

"So there were *rats* living in the walls of that last flat you went to?" Mum continues their conversation like she's forgotten I exist. "How *awful*! I would've run straight out and slammed the door!" She got dressed like she said she would and she's looking so much like her old self that for a minute I'm almost fooled. But something's wrong, flashing at me like a big warning light in the middle of the kitchen. Mum's face is glowing and her eyes go so sparkly every time she looks at Brian you'd think he was Santa Claus come to our flat at the wrong time of year.

I haven't seen her look like that since she met Rob, her last loser boyfriend. It was all wine and chocolates until Mum found out the police were after him for a load of car thefts round Glasgow. Before he left he gave Mum a black eye and nicked our telly. Seeing her look at Brian that way makes me want to throw up. There's no way I'm going to let her make *that* mistake again. Not when she's only just on the mend.

After a while Brian notices that I'm still standing there staring at him, and he starts putting his tools back in his bag.

"You're not going already?" Mum wails, trying to force-feed him the last of my chocolate digestives. I'm reaching for the empty biscuit tin to club him with, but he shakes his head and tells her he has another job to do before he can go home.

Mum trails after him to the door, and they have a hushed conversation that has Mum grinning from ear to ear by the time he finally leaves.

"What a nice man!" she sighs, staring at the door like she's considering running down the stairs and asking him to stay for dinner. "Don't you think he was nice Caylin?"

"He was just doing his job Mum, that's all it was," I mutter.

"Yes, he has such a nice smile," Mum nods like I'm the one who said it. "He's coming back tomorrow to have a look at the faulty lights in the Haddads' flat."

"Whose flat?" I'm only half-listening. I'm still staring at the empty biscuit tin and plotting revenge on Brian for eating my Saturday morning treat.

"The Haddads. You know, the refugee family downstairs? I was putting the washing on the line earlier and I met them coming back from the hospital."

"You *talked* to them?" I don't know what's weirder, the thought of Mum talking to Reema's mum and dad who don't speak English, or her doing the washing.

"Well, sort of. They had a translator with them. Mrs Haddad's so nice, I'll have to get her up here for a cup of tea some time. It's terrible what happened to them – they lost everything in the war. I said I'd put together a box of things to help them settle into their flat. We've got more of your grandad's plates and blankets cluttering up the place than we know what to do with. It's about time they were put to good use. I'll pack them up and take them down later. You don't mind, do you Caylin?"

Mum's trying to be cheerful about it, but I know the thought of letting go of her dad's stuff hurts her every bit as much as it hurts me. I clench my fists and look out of the window without answering. Mum takes that as a yes.

"I'm just going to have a quick shower now that it's fixed and then I'll make you something to eat. Is beans on toast OK for dinner tonight?"

"Sounds good." I manage a real smile this time. Mum hasn't made dinner in so long she could serve up a plate of deep-fried underpants and I'd think it was a banquet.

I'm reaching for the TV remote when Mum calls from the hall, "And don't put the TV on till after dinner! You watch way too much rubbish. Why don't you go and play with that new girl downstairs instead?"

She disappears into the bathroom before I can tell her I'd rather play with the motorway traffic than make friends with Reema. I don't want to say anything that will upset her though. I saw how pale her face was getting with the strain of all the talking she's done today and the way her smile was starting

79

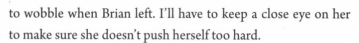

to wobble when Brian left. I'll have to keep a close eye on her to make sure she doesn't push herself too hard.

And that means keeping Brian as far away from her as possible.

I hurry to the kitchen and pull some of the hidden cans out from behind the biscuit tin, taking the chance to go and feed the foxes while Mum's in the bathroom. I need to be more careful this time so Poppy learns to trust me. She nearly bit me this morning when I reached out to touch her, but she was just looking out for her cubs.

I understand how she feels. I know what it's like to have someone I need to protect. I have sharp teeth too, and if that guy Brian comes near my mum again, he'll find out just how hard I can bite.

The Fox

Days come and go with the sun and the moonrise,
Turn into weeks as the spring buds unfurl.
   I wait for the moment when I can go hunting,
    For now I lie helpless, frustrated and weak.

   In the dark of the night I dream of escaping,
    Dream of a place that is green, wild and free.
    But my limp leg is shattered, my young ones are hungry.
   I must accept food from the two-legged beasts.

This One appears with the flickering dawn light,
That One arrives when the night closes in.
Other Ones come to the small-box by daylight,
Piling up bags full of waste and decay.

 Our hunger is fading but danger surrounds us,
   Eyes in the beast-box above us stare down.
    I huddle down lower. Hush, hush! Make no sound now.
    We must not be seen. We must not be heard.

   I cannot sleep,
    But I dream, I dream.
   No, I cannot sleep,
    But I *dream*.

12
Reema

In my dreams I still see the playground in Aleppo before the war. Sara and I are climbing into the seats of the mini Ferris wheel with a whole crowd of children from our apartment building, giggling with excitement as Jamal pushes us round and round.

"Higher Jamal, higher!" I yell, spinning so close to the sky that if I reach my hands up I can almost touch the edge of the sun. I look down to see Jamal pulling a face at me, crossing his eyes and sticking out his tongue. It makes me laugh so hard I almost fall from my seat as he spins us faster.

I do not feel like laughing today as I push Sara on the only swing in Drumhill that is not covered in graffiti.

I have not brought her to the park because the sun is shining for the first time since we arrived last month, or because the endless weeping rain has finally stopped. We are here because my parents were arguing and my father had a seizure, and I cannot bear to be at home right now.

"Higher Reema!" Sara cries, kicking her feet in the air and grinning from ear to ear. "Look! I am flying!"

Despite my heavy heart I smile at her delight. It has been so long since my last proper smile that my lips feel awkward and out of practice. "Any higher and you will turn into a bird and fly right back to Syria!" I try to make a joke.

Sara twists in her seat to look back at me, jerking the swing sideways. "I do not want to go back there Reema, not ever. They cannot make us leave here now, can they?"

Her face is suddenly so full of fear I catch her seat and slow it right down so she will not fall off. "We will stay here until the war is over *habibti*, and then we will go home, when it is safe to return. Would you not like that? To go home?"

"But we *are* home!" Sara frowns. "This is home. I have friends here – Jenny and Lauren and Claire – and I like my school, and I like sharing my bedroom with you, and I like our safe apartment, and I do not *want* to go back to Syria!"

Sara looks as though she is going to cry. I crouch down and hold her hand, trying to make her understand. "This is not our home, Sara. Syria is home. We are only here for a little while until our country is safe again. Do you not remember all the nice things we used to do? Remember when we used to go to the *souks* and help Mama with the shopping? How you used to love looking at all the pretty dresses and jewellery in the stalls?"

Sara shakes her head. "We did not go out. We hid in the house all the time from the bombs and the soldiers. It was so boring. Here we can go out whenever we want."

I try again. "Remember the food Aunt Amira used to make? The *tabouleh* salads and chicken *shawarma* and *baqlawa* pastries? And the *Eid al-Fitr* feast when we would invite all our family and friends to eat Mama's famous *ma'amoul* cookies?"

My mouth is watering at the very thought of my favourite dishes, but Sara is frowning at me as though I am speaking a foreign language.

"What are you talking about Reema? We were hungry all the time in Syria and at the refugee camp. There was never any food and the water was dirty. Now we can have pizza and chips and bread and soda whenever we like. I want to stay here forever."

Sara's words suck all of the air from my lungs until I am hollow and aching inside.

She has no idea what I am talking about. She is too young to remember all the good times our family had before the war. I spend every waking moment trying to hold on to my happy memories of Aleppo, picturing over and over the blue skies and market colours, the sounds of our calls to prayer and the smells of our spiced food. Sara remembers only bombs and snipers and the desperate hunger that ate us all up from the inside out.

My Syria is not her Syria, and never will be.

"Mama says we are staying here, so we *are* staying, are we not Reema? Even though Baba wants to go back to Syria, he cannot return now, can he? Not when he is so sick?"

Sara is looking half-doubtful, half-hopeful. She is still worried by Baba and Mama's big argument this morning when they thought we were still sleeping. Mama is angry that Baba is missing his hospital appointments and sits in the house all day and night on his phone. He spends so much time searching missing-person websites for Jamal that he forgets to eat, and he has not been to any of the English lessons at the community centre.

He does not even go to the mosque with us any more, and that is what worries me more than anything.

Mama wants to know what has happened to Jamal just as much as Baba does, but she is scared Baba will make himself ill with worry. That is why she shouts. It is not because she has forgotten Jamal, it is because remembering him is so painful.

It feels like our family is at war.

Jamal used to say that war is like a plague; you carry it with you wherever you go. The fighting has followed us even here, and our family is split down the middle. If only Jamal was here with us. Without him our family is broken.

"Reema? Will you push me again?" Sara is scuffing her shoes on the ground, bored by the talk of a country she does not remember. I nod and smile and swing her seat up again, but my heart is not in it now and my smile is no longer real.

Before I can lose myself in my memories of home, I see Caylin walking across the park. She is bringing a small boy who looks about Sara's age over to the swings. Her hands are buried in her pockets and her scowl is so deep it looks like it has been carved there with a knife.

"Hello," I try when the little boy runs over to sit on the swing and Caylin gives him an unenthusiastic push. "Is this… your brother?" I have not made any friends yet and English is hard, but Mama says I must practise if I want to be as good as Jamal. It is only the thought of seeing him again and making him proud of how much I have learned that makes me speak to this angry girl.

"No, don't be stupid." Caylin throws me a horrified look. "I haven't got a brother."

I have been sitting across the table from her in class for weeks now and I have started to understand the strange hissing way that she speaks, even though she only seems to argue with the boys at our table and to make excuses to the teacher for forgetting her homework. The other children in the playground avoid her, just like they avoid me. Her scowl frightens them away just like my headscarf does.

"This is … my sister… Sara," I try again.

"Duh." Caylin rolls her eyes. This seems to be her favourite word.

"I'm Johnny," the boy says, reaching into his pocket and pulling out a packet of candy. "You want a bubblegum?"

I shake my head when he offers me a sweet, but Sara reaches over and takes one, and soon he is showing her how to blow bubbles and they are chatting away, the swings forgotten. Sara is picking up English much faster than I am, and she is not embarrassed to make mistakes. The other children at school have warmed to her just like this boy has, and she already has friends to play with after school. I try not to be envious of how quickly she is fitting in. This is not my country. I do not need to belong here.

"Why do you wear that stupid thing?"

"Sorry?" I realise that Caylin is actually speaking to me. I try not to sound surprised.

"That tea towel on your head. What's it for?"

I frown when I work out what a tea towel is. Then I bite my tongue and count to three like Mama says I should before snapping a reply I might regret. "It is called … *hijab*. Women in … my country… wearing them to… cover… their hairs."

"Yeah, but *why?*"

"Em…" I hesitate for a long moment, trying to think of all the English words I need to explain why I like to wear my *hijab* even though I do not need to. How can I describe to a stranger in a foreign language what this sea-green scarf means to me and how much I miss my brother and my home?

Then I realise Caylin is not staring at my scarf. It is the long braid underneath that she is gazing at. There is admiration and more than a little envy in her eyes. She is not asking me why I wear a headscarf, she is asking me why I cover my long hair.

I pull out my braid and show it to her. "It… needing… cut," I smile. Mama always used to trim the split ends to keep it neat, but she has not done it for a long time.

"No!" Caylin looks so alarmed at the thought that I cannot help laughing. "Don't cut it off. It's too pretty." She snaps her mouth shut and turns away as soon as she has said it, frowning as though she regrets the compliment. She has given me a way in though, and I make sure I pull the door wide open before she can close it in my face.

"I like… your hairs… also," I say. "It is nice."

"It's horrible." Caylin grabs a strand of shaggy hair that has fallen over her face and tries to run a finger through it, showing me how tangled it is. She knows I am not being truthful. She is not the sort of girl who likes being lied to.

"No," I try again, "I mean, I like… the colour. Brown and red… just like… a fox." The words are out before I realise I have said them. I could not help it – her hair is almost the same colour as Hurriyah's rusty fur. I hold my breath, hoping she will not take this as an insult.

Instead of frowning though, her eyes light up and she smiles at me. "You think so?" She sounds doubtful but pleased.

I nod. "Same colour."

She grins, and for a few moments I feel as though I have finally made a friend. But then the sunshine in her eyes is hidden behind the dark cloud of her brows as she scowls again.

I see she is not frowning at me though, and I look over my shoulder. There is a man walking across the grass, with a big dog on a lead. He is passing near the swings when he looks round and notices us. His eyes come to rest on my *hijab*, and the anger I see there makes my blood run cold.

13
Caylin

I thought today couldn't possibly get any worse, but I was wrong.

It started out bad enough, with that stupid electrician Brian taking Mum out for lunch and leaving me to babysit his unbelievably annoying kid.

If I wasn't so mad with them both I'd remember they wanted me to come too, but there was no way I was going play happy families with Mum's new loser boyfriend. I kicked a tantrum and told Mum I'd rather see her drown in a bottle of vodka than go all gooey again over some muppet she's only just met. That's when she packed me off to the park with Johnny and told me not to come back till I'd cooled off and made friends with the wee troll.

I could be here for a very long time.

Johnny's every bit as dumb as he looks. He's eight and he still can't tie his own shoelaces, and his nose runs so much he's like a leaky tap someone's forgotten to turn off. It's totally minging. Thank God Brian only has him at the weekends and he stays with his mum and stepdad the rest of the week. This is the one and only time I'm looking after him though. I don't want Mum thinking I'm OK with her seeing Brian and that I don't mind getting stuck with his idiot son.

Not only do I have to waste my time pushing Johnny on the swings and talking to Reema when I'd rather be with my foxes, now there's someone storming across the park towards us who makes every frizzy hair on my head stand on end.

Darren Bradshaw's out of prison again, and it looks like he's got his big Doberman back off whoever was looking after it while he was away. That's the dog that bit me a few years ago, only the police couldn't prove it so it was never put down. It's a vicious thing, and its owner isn't any better. Darren's had it in for me ever since the police went round to his flat asking about his dog.

Darren's eyes narrow when he gets closer, but then he sees Reema's headscarf and he stops dead, his face twisting up like he's about to explode. When he's not in prison doing time for breaking into houses or beating people up, he's down the pub or the chip shop giving off to anyone who'll listen about foreigners coming here and taking over our country. My stomach knots in fear and I take a step back, bumping into Johnny's swing.

"What the hell's a wee towel-head terrorist doing in my park, eh?" he yells, tugging on the lead so hard his dog starts growling and snapping at the air. "You here to blow up wee kids while they're out playing, is that it?"

Reema glances at me, fear in her eyes. She doesn't understand anything he's saying, but she can see he's angry and probably dangerous. I know I should help her, but I'm too scared. I keep my mouth shut and edge further away, grabbing Johnny's arm and hissing that it's time to go. He takes one look at the growling

91

dog and decides he's had enough fun at the park for one day. I take off, pulling Johnny behind me as I leg it across the grass as fast as my feet will go.

"Why don't you go back to the tent in the desert where you came from, eh? Instead of coming here and living off benefits that other people work for? Get out of here, or I'll set my dog on you!"

Reema might not understand what Darren's shouting, but she understands what he means alright. She takes her wee sister's hand and chases after me, shouting at me to wait for them. I ignore her. I remember what it felt like to be bitten by the dog that's snarling at the end of Darren's lead, and my heart's beating too fast for me to think straight.

Even though I got a head start, we reach the park gates together.

I don't have time to be surprised at how quick Reema is though. Darren's still behind us, grinning so hard the world can see his missing teeth. We keep on running down the street towards our block of flats, Darren's insults following us all the way.

"Don't come here again you wee Muslim terrorists, or my dog'll eat the whole lot of you!"

I don't look back at Reema and Sara as we run into our building. I just clamp my hand round Johnny's arm so hard I nearly break his bones as I drag him up the stairs to the safety of the flat. It's only when the door's shut firmly behind us and the security chain is on that I realise I should've checked to make sure Reema's parents were in or she had a key. I'm too scared to go back now though. My legs are shaking too hard for me to get down the stairs without falling.

Just when I think there's no way I could feel any worse, Johnny asks, "Do you think Reema and Sara are OK?" His bottom lip's trembling, and I feel like slapping his snotty wee face for making me feel so guilty.

"They're fine," I snap. "Go and put the telly on. And don't start bubbling or I won't make you any toast!"

But it's me who's nearly crying. I should've stuck up for Reema and her wee sister. They didn't understand what Darren was saying, but I did. I should've told him where to stick his insults and his big mangy dog. But I didn't. I just ran away like a coward.

If Grandad had been at the park with me there's no way Darren would've dared to open his big mouth. I miss him so much right now I feel sick. I close my eyes, holding on to the back of the sofa and trying to remember a much happier visit to a much better park. If I think really hard about that picture in the album under my pillow, sometimes I see flashes of the day we fed the squirrels at Ravensholm.

All of a sudden it's like I'm right there in the photo, and forgotten memories come flooding back.

It's summer, and I'm wearing the new shorts and T-shirt Gran and Grandad got for my birthday. The sun is shining and the wind is whispering in the trees, daring me to try to catch it. I'm running through the entrance gates up the hill to the water fountain on my stumpy wee legs, trying to win the race and get there first.

"Caylin, wait for me!"

I can hear a voice behind me. I think it's Gran's. Even though my legs are so short I can't even reach our front door handle, Gran's pretending I'm too fast for her. I make it to the wee metal fountain first, squirting water high into the air and watching the droplets sparkle in the sunlight.

I turn to look at the woman running up the hill towards me, and that's when my memory goes dark, her face blurring and fading back into the distant past.

"Caylin, wait for me!"

A voice calls again, but it's not Gran's, it's Reema's. She's running through Drumhill Park behind me with her wee sister, trying to get away from Darren and his dog. She doesn't understand what he's saying to her and she doesn't understand why I've just run away and left her behind.

It's not my job to look out for her! I tell myself, stomping into the kitchen and clattering the toaster and banging the cupboard doors as hard as I can. But no matter how much noise I make, I can't chase away the memory of Reema's scared eyes staring after me, full of hurt and disappointment.

14
Reema

"I do not want to go to English class today!" Sara is wailing, clinging on to the door handle with both hands. She was beginning to settle here in Glasgow, to relax. Until that bad man and his dog chased us in the park yesterday.

"Sara, enough of this, the taxi has been waiting outside for ten minutes," Mama snaps. "The Refugee Council will stop paying if it leaves without us."

Our trips to the community centre and mosque where we can meet up with other refugees and immigrants who speak our language are very important to her.

"Leave the girl be," Baba sighs. "It will not matter if you miss one class."

"And then we will miss the next class, and the next," Mama says angrily. "It is your example she is following! If you would only come and learn English with us then—"

"I do not need language classes!" Baba interrupts her. "Once the war is over we will go back to Syria, and what will be the point of all those English lessons then, eh?"

95

I think Baba is just making excuses not to leave the house, but Mama rolls her eyes, ready for another argument.

"The war might go on for many years yet. You cannot just sit here waiting for Jamal to come home so he can translate for us!"

We all go silent.

Sara lets go of the door handle and clutches Mama's hand instead.

"Is Jamal coming home?" she asks hopefully. "Has he been found?"

The colour drains from Baba's face. He turns without a word and shuffles back down the hall to his bedroom, leaning heavily on the crutches the hospital is teaching him to use. The hard look goes out of Mama's eyes and they become soft as *labneh* yoghurt. I want to hug her, but I am afraid it will make her cry.

"Not yet *habibti*." Mama strokes Sara's hair sadly. "Now come to your English class with no more fuss and let your father rest."

Sara puts on her coat reluctantly, her bottom lip quivering. "But Reema is not going. Can I not stay home with her?"

"Reema has a headache, she needs to rest this afternoon," Mama says, handing me two aspirin tablets to take with the water I am sipping. "Tira Hamed has promised to bring some *phyllo* dough to class to give me today, so I will make your favourite *baqlawa* for supper tonight when you feel better, yes?" Mama strokes my brow and gives me a worried smile.

I smile back as they leave, but it is a guilty smile. I do not have a headache. That is not why I do not want to go to the class with them. I am not sick, I am just too angry to learn English today.

"Stupid language!" I mutter, watching from the window as the taxi drives away down the street. My eyes follow Sara's pale face until the car turns the corner and disappears. "Stupid country. Stupid food. Stupid weather. Stupid school. Stupid, STUPID people!"

I bang my fist down on the coffee table so hard I hear one of the legs crack.

"Stupid second-hand junk!"

I shove the table against the wall so it does not fall over, and take a deep breath. It does not help. I am so angry I want to scream, but I cannot in case Baba hears. I did not tell my parents about the man in the park, as it would only upset them. I told them Sara was crying because she fell over and hurt herself. I do not know what that man was shouting, but it was clear he does not want me and my family to be here.

"Stupid man!" I growl, remembering the way his eyes narrowed when he saw my *hijab* and his face twisting up with hate. "I do not want to be in your stupid country any more than you want me to be here."

If only I could go back to Syria, the way it was before the war.

If only I could go *home*.

There is only one thing here that I care about, one thing that makes me happy, and that is Hurriyah and her cubs.

I go to the kitchen and fill a small plastic bag with scraps from the fridge and an empty bottle with milk, and carry them to the door. I usually feed Hurriyah after dark when my family has gone to bed, but today I will not be seen slipping out early with her food.

97

I open the door a crack and check to make sure Mrs Mitchell has not come back from her coffee club yet. Her door is still closed, so she is not at home. I am not sure what Caylin does after school, but I have never seen her out playing with other children before yesterday in the park, so she is probably watching TV with her mother. Our neighbours on the second floor do not come back from work until early evening, and I have never met the other couple on the top floor.

It is safe. I will not be seen.

I hurry down the corridor and step out into the back garden. It is late April now and the sun will not set for several hours yet. The ground is still muddy even though it has not rained all week, so I stick to the narrow path and make my way carefully down to the small trash shed. I do not want to bring mud back into the house and make my parents suspicious. I would love to tell Sara, but my little sister cannot keep a secret to herself for even five minutes. She would burst with excitement and tell the whole world about the foxes living at the bottom of the garden, and then something bad might happen to them.

Hurriyah and her cubs must remain a secret.

My secret.

"Sshh, it is only me, there is no need to be afraid," I whisper, as Hurriyah gives her usual warning snarl when I peek round the back of the shed. Her cubs are getting bigger and their eyes have opened now. At first they were blue, but now they have changed to a beautiful amber that glows in the sunlight when they wake from their sleep. Hurriyah growls and tries to stop them coming to greet me, snapping and pushing them back when I bend down,

98

but she is stiff and sore, and her leg will not support her. She is having trouble making them obey her now that they are able to move around by themselves.

I fill the plastic bowls I keep hidden under a box nearby and push them forward, careful not to let the cubs come too near me. Baba would not like it, and neither would Hurriyah. She waits to make sure I will keep my distance from her cubs, then she leans down and nudges them gently aside, making room for herself at the big bowl of food.

I cannot help smiling to myself as I lean against the wall and watch them eat. Mama is starting to wonder where all of our leftover food is disappearing to, but Baba just laughs when he finds the fridge empty and says that Sara and I are making up for all those years of hunger. He likes to think that his children's bellies are full now that we are safe.

But are the foxes safe? I wonder. What if someone sees them? What if someone thinks they don't belong here any more than me and my family do? Who would help them if they were found one day when I was not here to save them?

Not Caylin, that is certain.

Caylin did not help me and Sara in the park when that man was threatening us. She just ran away. She does not care how bad he made us feel.

She is not my friend.

I am so busy thinking about the mean girl upstairs that at first I do not notice there are only four cubs around the food bowl. I move a little closer and peer behind the shed, seeing the fifth one curled up on the ground by the wall. He is not asleep, but he is not moving either. He looks small and weak, and he pants as though breathing is an effort. I have noticed him hanging back at feeding time before, but I thought he would get stronger as the days passed. He has not. Even his fur has not got lighter and redder like the rest of the cubs, and he is missing the red and white face patches of the others. It is as though he is getting smaller instead of growing up with the rest.

"Come on little one, you have to eat," I tell him, scooping a handful of rice and meat scraps from the bottom of the bag and forming it into a little ball that I throw behind the shed. The rice ball lands right in front of him, but he just sniffs it wearily and closes his eyes again without tasting it.

My heart beats painfully as I watch and I am afraid I am going to cry. This little one will not grow. He is too weak. I do not know how to help him.

The other cubs have finished the food already and are sniffing around for more. Mama will be away for several hours, so I will risk bringing them more food.

I pick up the bowls, but when I turn round I let out a cry of surprise. There is someone standing right behind me, someone with a scowl so fierce I can almost hear her growling.

15
Caylin

"What the hell are you doing here?" It's out of my mouth before I remember that's exactly what Darren with the dog yelled at her. I don't care. Poppy is *my* fox, and I'm so angry when I see the food bowls she's holding I want to punch her lights out.

"Are you trying to poison them or something? Poppy and her cubs don't want your minging foreign food!"

I knock the bowls from her hand, dropping one of my tins in the process, and out-of-date meatballs go slopping over the path. One of the cubs darts forward ready to scoop them up, but Poppy's head shoots out from behind the shed and she grabs the cub in her jaws, dragging him away.

"Poppy?" Reema catches hold of one of the few words she made out from my super-fast shouting. "What is 'poppy'?"

"It's her name!" I snap. "The name of *my* fox. Leave her alone! If I ever see you out here again I swear I'll—"

"Her name is Hurriyah!"

Reema says it slowly and clearly, stepping right up to me and standing toe to toe so there'll be no mistaking her meaning. I'm not used to this from kids my age. Most of them are scared

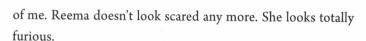

of me. Reema doesn't look scared any more. She looks totally furious.

For the first time I don't know what to do.

"What's that supposed to mean?" I mutter, playing for time.

"It means 'freedom'. It is her name. The name of *my* fox."

"Poppy is *mine*!" I yell. Then I remember that Mrs Mitchell will be back from her coffee club any minute and will come straight out here to stick her nose in if she hears any shouting. I lower my voice and hiss, "This is my country, not yours, and this fox belongs here with me. You don't." I say it clearly, just like she did. I want to make sure she understands every word.

"You also do not belong here," she shoots straight back. She stumbles over the words but she keeps on going. "No one likes you. You have no friends. It is you who must go. You steal food and it makes the little one sick. Stealing is *haram*! It is forbidden! The little one is paying for your badness. Because of you he is dying! It is your fault!"

She leans in so close I can see flecks of light in her furious brown eyes. Her angry words hit me like a blow to the gut.

Before I even know what I'm doing I take a step back. "It wasn't stolen!" I say weakly, all the fight knocked out of me. "I didn't…" I trail off. Reema's seen me in the Spar hanging round the tinned food more than once now. All that time I thought she was struggling to read the labels she was looking at me sideways with those suspicious eyes of hers, watching me steal and judging me for it. She's probably been waiting for this moment to catch me with my stolen tins so she can go and tell on me.

But if she spills my secret, then she'll give Poppy and her cubs away too. I can't let that happen.

"If you open your mouth to anyone, and I mean *ANYONE*," I begin, "then I'll... Wait. What do you mean the wee one's sick and is going to die?"

I know the smallest cub's not as strong as the rest, but he just needs a bit more time to grow, I'm sure of it. I have to repeat the question before Reema understands, but when she does she grabs me roughly by the arm and pulls me over to the wall, pointing behind the shed at the wee ball of fur curled up behind Poppy and the four bigger cubs.

"Look!" she snaps. "That one is sick. He is not eating, only sleeping. I do not know what to do."

"Well, maybe if you weren't feeding him your weird foreign food—" I begin again, and then stop, freezing when I hear a familiar noise. From the other end of the close comes the sound of metal clanging. Someone's walking up the wheelchair ramp. Someone with a walking stick.

Reema glances at me, her eyes narrowing.

"Mrs Mitchell!" I hiss.

She nods. She's not stupid, even if she can't speak English properly. She knows the old witch is a danger to Poppy and her cubs. If Mrs Mitchell sees us out here with food and bowls she'll want to know what we're up to. And she won't rest until she finds out exactly what's going on behind the bin shed.

"Hide it!" Reema whispers, pointing to the overturned box by the side fence. I shove my tins and bottle underneath, kicking Reema's plastic bowls under too, and wait, listening hard.

The footsteps have stopped in the close and a key turns in a lock. Mrs Mitchell is a bit deaf. As long as we don't make any loud noises she'll never know we're back here.

Just when I think we're safe, the biggest cub comes bounding out from behind the bin shed. She waddles up to the puddle of spilt meatballs and gravy and starts licking at it. Reema takes a step back like she's trying to avoid touching the cub, and trips over one of the bags the upstairs neighbours have left by the side of the shed. Before I can grab her she falls back against the bins, knocking them over like a row of dominos.

It's like watching a film in slow motion, but I can't reach the remote to press pause. The bins tip over, the last one making a big booming sound as it hits the ground and spills its bags. Even half-deaf Mrs Mitchell with her faulty hearing aid can't miss the noise.

Reema scrambles up and tries to tidy the mess she's made, but it's too late for that now. "Hide!" I tell her. I grab the fox cub by the scruff of the neck and race behind the shed, squeezing into the gap between the back of the shed and the wall. The cub is trying to bite me, her wee teeth nipping at my hand, so I put her down next to her mother, hoping Poppy'll stop growling before Mrs Mitchell comes out.

Reema ducks behind the bin shed too, trying to keep away from the cubs that are clambering over Poppy to see why there are big people stomping all over their bedroom. I don't know what her problem is with touching the foxes. It's not like they're going to give her the plague or anything. I wouldn't be sorry if they did though.

I put my finger to my lips to make sure she knows to keep her mouth shut, and peer round the side of the shed. Mrs Mitchell is coming down the steps into the garden, her eyes blinking like an owl behind her NHS specs and her face twitching like she's trying to sniff out the secrets she knows must be hiding here. When I duck back out of sight and hold my breath I can hear her tutting and sighing over the mess. There's a series of thumps as she tries to right the bins, but she can't manage the weight with her walking stick and weak knee and gives up. As she shuffles away I can hear her muttering something about the Council and her selfish neighbours.

My stomach is doing somersaults, and when I glance over at Reema I can see her jaw clenched tight with nerves too. She doesn't understand what Mrs Mitchell is saying about the Council though. She doesn't know that if the old bat gets someone round about the bins, the first thing they'll find is Poppy and her cubs hiding behind the shed. Reema doesn't understand any of that.

I understand though. Only I can keep them safe.

We wait until the coast is clear and edge back out into the garden. I don't look at Reema as I grab the tins and bottle from under the box and empty them into the bowls I've kept hidden behind a bush. I don't need Reema's permission to feed my foxes. She stands there with her arms folded, and I'm sure as I bend down with the bowls I can feel her eyes drilling into my back. But when I turn round I see it's the smallest fox curled up at the back of the group that she's looking at. Her eyes aren't angry any more, they're just sad.

I won't let myself feel sad though. The wee one isn't hungry tonight, that's all. He'll be hungry tomorrow morning, and I'll make sure he eats a double helping. I'll pick him up and stroke him and cuddle him and feed him by hand if I have to. Reema wouldn't do that. She doesn't really care about the foxes.

She doesn't even want to touch them.

When I turn round again to tell her she should go away, I find she's already gone. The insults I had ready die on my tongue. I'll keep them stored up though, ready for next time. There's no way I'm going to let her get the better of me in an argument ever again.

The Fox

Spring passes slowly, I grow ever restless.
My body is fragile, my leg does not heal.
 The hunger is gone, instead fear gnaws my belly,
   Bites at my insides by night and by day.

   With no den to hide them, my young are not safe here.
   I cannot protect them or teach them to hunt.
   One through to Four are now milk-weaned and active.
   But Five is my worry, too helpless, too weak.

 He sleeps through the night while the others are playing,
His eyes growing dimmer with each passing dawn.
I chew up his meat; he has no strength to swallow,
My other ones take it, so then he has none.

Soon he will leave us.
Goodbye to my youngest.
 Yes, soon he will leave us.
   Goodbye.

16
Reema

The sun is shining brightly for the first time since I arrived in this country, and I am lost in dreams of home again. It is not the houses of Drumhill I see glinting in the sunlight, it is the yellow and white stones of the great Citadel in Aleppo that shimmer in the afternoon heat.

"Come on!" I call back to Baba and Jamal as I run up the broad steps to the inner gate. "You are too slow!"

My legs are short and I am tired from the long walk through the *souks* to get here, but I will not admit it. I want Baba to think I am strong like him, and to show Jamal I am not a baby who must stay at home like little Sara. I pass under the great archway, my breath coming in short gasps. I can almost feel the weight of the huge stone tower pressing down on my head. I keep running, chasing the shafts of sunlight from the narrow windows all the way to the very top. When I am outside, on the massive Citadel rooftop surrounded by the historic ruins of palace buildings, domes and outdoor theatre, I finally stop, my lungs ready to burst. Before I can catch my breath I am swept up in Baba's arms, and he lifts me onto his broad shoulders, carrying me over to the wall where we can look out across the city.

"Oh! It is so beautiful!" I gasp. "I can see the whole world!"

Aleppo stretches far off to the distant horizon in every direction. The furthest houses and towers and mosques I can make out in the haze are so far away that they are too small even for Sara's dolls to live in.

"The world is much bigger than our city, Little Gazelle," Jamal laughs. "Maybe one day when you are bigger you will go and see more of it."

"No," I shake my head so hard I nearly fall from Baba's shoulders, "I will never leave here. Aleppo is my home."

My home.

"Reema, did you catch all that? Do you understand what we're doing today?" our gym teacher Miss Lindsey asks me, interrupting my daydreams.

All we have to do is run round the school. It is not difficult.

I open my eyes again, but it is not my home that I see now. It is a school playground in a strange city that surrounds me. I cannot see to the horizon. The tower blocks are so high I cannot even see to the edge of the Drumhill estate. It makes me feel dizzy to think of the distance dividing me from the country where I was born.

"Remember, everyone," Miss Lindsey says to the class, "I'll be starting the sports club in a few weeks, and later this term we'll have trials to see who will represent Drumhill in the Glasgow schools athletics competition. I hope you'll all come along to our practice sessions and try out for your school team."

I listen hard, trying to follow her words, my heart beating with excitement when I work out what she is saying.

A running competition? That will finally give me the chance to show my classmates I am good at something!

I think our class teacher Mrs Gibb has mentioned this before, but she speaks so fast that many times I do not understand her, and she does not always have the patience to repeat her instructions slowly for me. I hate feeling lost and confused when she gives us a task I do not know how to complete. It makes me look stupid, and I know I am not.

Not like Caylin.

Last night I looked up the English name 'Poppy' in the dictionary.

It is a kind of flower that is grown in the Middle East. It can be turned into a drug that makes money for fighters to keep their wars going. Caylin has named my fox after something pretty that causes misery for my people.

She is so stupid it would make me laugh if I was not so angry.

I glance across the playground at her, but she is not looking my way. She is too busy glaring at Lisa from our class, who bumped into her at lunchtime and made her drop her tray of food on the floor. I think Lisa did it on purpose, and the other students were all laughing. Caylin still has bits of yoghurt on her socks, but we have changed into our gym clothes, so at least she does not have to wear her sweatshirt and trousers that are covered in gravy and jelly.

I think she is still embarrassed, but I do not feel bad for her.

She deserves it. She—

A shrill blast sounds so loud in my ears I almost scream in fright.

The bombing has started again!

I drop to my knees, covering my head with my hands like Baba showed us when the planes carrying barrel bombs passed above our house.

I thought we were safe here! My mind is crying over and over, *I thought we were safe!*

My heart is pounding and my hands reach automatically for my headscarf. It is my lucky charm, the one thing that still links me to the big brother who always kept me safe. My fingers find only my hair braid though, and I remember that Miss Lindsey asked me to take my scarf off for gym class. It is strange, but now I feel naked and unprotected without it. It is as though Jamal has left me here all alone, facing the bombs by myself.

"Reema?" Miss Lindsey sounds concerned.

I raise my head and risk looking up. Miss Lindsey is standing over me, a worried look on her face. "Reema, what's the matter? Did this give you a fright?" She holds up the whistle she has just blown.

At first I feel a warm rush of relief, but as I stand up on shaky legs the heat grows until my cheeks are burning in embarrassment. The other students are disappearing round the side of the building, jostling and racing each other to see who will make the long lap of the school building first. Only Caylin is left at the back, jogging slowly and looking as though she is making no effort at all.

"I'm sorry Reema, I should have warned you first." Miss Lindsey pats me on the shoulder gently. "If you'd like to sit down and—"

"No, I am fine," I say quickly, breaking into a run before her kind words and concern make the tears in my eyes spill out. I feel stupid, and hope none of my classmates saw what I did. I do not want pity and sympathy from anyone any more.

I just want to prove that I am fast.

I round the corner at top speed and see that the other children are already way ahead. Caylin has been left far behind, plodding along so slowly she is barely moving faster than a tortoise.

I can outrun her easily.

Our eyes meet as I pass her, and something in her face changes. The sullen, bored look disappears, and instead of overtaking her, I suddenly find myself struggling to keep up. I grit my teeth and draw level with her again, but she gallops on ahead and it is all I can do to keep on her heels.

The sideways grin she throws me as she pulls away makes my blood boil.

The other children are out of sight round the side of the school, and Miss Lindsey cannot see us. It is only me and Caylin here, tearing through the junior playground, running as though our lives depend on it.

We both have something to prove, and I will not let her beat me.

I dig deep, remembering the races I used to run with Jamal through the streets of Aleppo after school. With my head uncovered, the wind streaming through my hair seems to carry the noises of home from far, far away. I can hear the sound of taxis and buses honking their horns in the afternoon traffic, the calls of traders selling their snacks and cool drinks by the side of the road, and the laughter of children playing hopscotch in the alleyways they have covered with chalk. No one can catch me, not even Jamal.

I am Reema, the White Gazelle, and I was born to run.

I search deep in my memories and find my rhythm, my legs eating up the distance until I am right on Caylin's shoulder. She glances over and I can see the strain on her face. She has speed, but now she is tired.

She does not have my stamina.

I overtake her on the bend and our classmates come back into view just ahead of us. We have run so fast we have caught the group again. As I race on past them, I realise Caylin is no longer with me. She has dropped back, jogging carelessly at the tail end of the last group once more. She clearly does not want our gym teacher and the other children to know she is good at running. I do not know why. She has no other talents.

I am at the front now, only two tall boys ahead of me. They are huffing and panting as we round the final corner of the school and we can see Miss Lindsey again. I can tell she is surprised to see me so near the front, but I am not content to come in third. I clench my fists hard, my arms pumping by my sides, willing myself forward over the last twenty metres.

The boys are left trailing behind, and I cross the chalk finish line Miss Lindsey has drawn on the ground in first place.

I have won. I have proved to them all that I am the White Gazelle, and I am fast.

Caylin may be faster than me over a short distance, but that is alright, because I am stronger.

I will always outrun her in the end.

17
Caylin

I totally beat her. If Miss Lindsey hadn't made us run a stupid marathon instead of a straight race then I would've crossed the finish miles ahead of Reema.

It wasn't a fair contest.

I'm just glad no one else saw it. Back in the junior classes I used to love sports, but ever since Grandad died I've been pretending I can't run to save my life. All Mum ever goes on about is how good a runner Gran was and how I'm so like her. She keeps saying I'm going to make her proud by winning competitions and running for Scotland, and I'm so scared to disappoint her I'd rather not try in the first place.

Anyway, after all the bullying I've done for money, the other kids are looking for any excuse to make fun of me. I've already got a big target painted on my back because of my lisp and smelly clothes. There's no way I'm going to draw any more attention to myself by beating the other kids at PE and making them hate me even more.

As long as I know I can outrun Reema, that's all that matters.

I see her waiting at the school railings for her wee sister to come out, and I take the shortcut home through the alleys behind the blocks of flats. I want to get back and see Poppy and her cubs before Reema turns up. The smallest one was looking a wee bit better this morning and ate some corned beef out of my hand, so now I don't feel so bad about the tins I've been pinching from the Spar.

Brian's nagged Mum into going to a therapy group for folk who drink too much, so she won't be home till five, and Mrs Mitchell's out at her coffee and gossip club down at the community centre. I'm expecting the coast to be clear for me to nip outside and check on the foxes, but when I get back Reema's mum is coming down the wheelchair ramp with another woman in a headscarf who I don't recognise.

"Hello Caylin."

"Hello Mrs Haddad," I mumble back. I'm a bit scared of Reema's mum. She's tall and beautiful and has the kind of big dark eyes that seem to look right through you and see all your darkest secrets without NHS X-ray specs. Even Mrs Mitchell behaves herself around Mrs Haddad. But today her dark eyes are sad and she looks as though she's been crying. I guess she's had another argument with Reema's dad. Mum's been down to visit them a couple of times now. She says Mr Haddad is missing home and finding it hard being sick all the time.

I hope Mum doesn't make friends with Mrs Haddad. That'd make it even harder for me to avoid her pain-in-the-bum daughter.

I nip up to my kitchen to spoon corned beef into the plastic bowls I use for the foxes, carrying them back down carefully and checking to make sure no one is about before I sneak into the garden. Poppy usually sleeps during the day, but sometimes I see the cubs playing round the yard while the sun's still up. It always makes me nervous, even though they run back behind the shed every time they hear footsteps. One of these days they're going to be seen by someone other than me and Reema, and then there'll be trouble.

The garden is quiet today though, and the foxes are nowhere to be seen.

When I peer round the back of the shed I'm met by Poppy's familiar warning growl. She looks more wary than usual today. The four bigger cubs are fast asleep, but they wake as soon as they smell the meat I've brought. They eat greedily, growling at each other and whimpering when Poppy pushes them aside with her nose to get at the food.

But one of them is missing; I can't see the smallest cub behind the shed.

I search around the garden, behind bushes, under abandoned boxes and behind the rubbish bins. There's no sign of him, right up until I turn over one of the black plastic bags by the back wall.

That's when I see him.

He's all curled up and he isn't moving, and even before I stroke his fur and feel how cold he is, I know he's dead.

My whole chest collapses like someone's squeezed all the air out of me, and I don't have any breath left to cry out. My legs are shaking and I sink to my knees, getting mud and grass stains all over my school trousers. I don't care. I don't care about anything other than this wee scrap of fur and bones. I was supposed to keep him safe but I couldn't.

I don't even know I'm crying until I open my eyes and see a big wet patch of snot and tears on my jumper. I wipe my face with my sleeve, not even minding the smell of stale yoghurt that Lisa spilled all over me at lunchtime. Getting revenge on Zoe and Lisa for that doesn't matter any more. Nothing matters. I had a fox and five cubs to look after and now there are only four and a big hole where the last one should be. I feel so helpless I could scream.

"What am I going to do?" I whisper, stroking the wee dead cub's fur with trembling fingers. "What do I do now?"

"We must put it in the ground."

I spin round, biting back a yell of fright. Reema's standing behind me, a big fat tear running down her face. She doesn't wipe it away like I do. She isn't ashamed like I am. Maybe she thinks it's my fault this wee fox died too.

"What are you doing here?" I snap, trying to sound more in control than I feel. "I thought I made it clear you're not welcome here."

Reema isn't angry with me today though. She doesn't want to fight back, she just wants to see the foxes. She bends down and looks at the cub sadly. "We must put it in the ground, so other animals do not get it."

"Bury it?" I ask. It seems wrong. Maybe if we just wait long enough he'll wake up again and everything will be alright.

"*Bury*…" Reema repeats the word as though testing it, and then nods. "Yes, that is what we must do."

Before I can reply she hurries away, and I think she's left me to it. I crouch there by the tiny body, feeling small and lost.

I don't want to be on my own right now. When Grandad died, I remember sitting up on his bed after the funeral, listening to the grown-ups all talking together downstairs and feeling like nothing would ever be right with the world again. I've felt like that ever since.

"Reema?" I call, then wait. There's no reply.

Poppy and the other foxes are looking at me from behind the shed, but the cubs don't come out to me like they usually do. They can smell death, and they're every bit as scared of it as I am.

"Here, cover him with this."

Before I can start to cry again Reema's back, handing me an old sheet. She starts to scoop at the ground by the back wall with a piece of broken wood, digging a wee grave for us to bury the fox. There are still tears in her eyes, but her face is hard and determined, and for once I'm alright with her taking charge and telling me what to do.

I guess she's seen so much death in her country's war it doesn't frighten her any more.

When I've finished wrapping the wee fox in the sheet I place him in the hole that Reema's dug, and she starts covering him with soil and patting it down with the length of wood. When she's done, she sticks the wood into the ground against the back wall so we'll know where we put him. To anyone else it'll just look like the end of a plank that's been thrown away, but we'll know what it means.

It'll be our secret.

"I didn't even give him a name," I say sadly, biting back the big lump in my throat. "It isn't right he died without a name."

"We must give them all names," Reema says, "all of Hurriyah's cubs."

"Her name is Poppy," I insist, the familiar anger rising again. "I found her first."

"No, I am the one who is feeding her first. She is hungry before I am feeding her." Reema's stumbling over her words in her haste to get them out, but I can still understand what she's saying, and it makes me mad.

"The foxes are in my garden!" I yell.

"They are outside my apartment!" Reema throws straight back, pointing to the small bedroom windows looking out onto the yard.

This is my country! Go home! I'm about to yell out loud, but then I remember Darren and his dog in the park and the way his angry words made Reema's little sister cry even though she didn't understand them. I take a deep breath and say instead, "Look, we'll toss a coin for it, OK? Heads it's Poppy, tails it's Hurryiyayeah or whatever you call her, agreed?"

Reema frowns, and I can tell she doesn't get it. I take a ten-pence coin from my pocket and show her both sides, pointing to heads and saying Poppy, and pointing to tails and garbling the word I think she's been using.

"*Hurriyah,*" she corrects me.

"Yeah, whatever, agreed?"

Reema nods.

"One throw and it's decided, no going back or changing it, OK?" I say. "Then there'll be no more arguments."

"No more arguments." Reema likes the sound of that.

If I felt like smiling after all the tears I've just cried, then I'd smile now. I know how to toss a coin to make sure it always comes up heads. There's a special flick you can put on it to send it into the air, and if you catch it just right on the way down it'll always land on the side you want. It was just about the only useful thing I ever learned from Mum's last boyfriend, Rob.

I toss the coin into the air just the way he showed me, but my hands are shaking and I don't throw it right. On the way down it slips between my fingers and lands on the ground. "Oops," I mutter, bending down to pick it up. "Rubbish throw. I'll need to do it again."

"No." Reema puts her foot over the coin before I can touch it. "One throw and it is decided. No more arguments, you said so."

"Yeah, but I didn't…" I trail off. She's right. If I go back on this now then we'll never agree on anything ever again. And if we're going to keep the foxes safe and make sure none of the other cubs die of hunger, we'll have to work together.

"OK fine," I mutter. "What is it, heads or tails?"

There's a sinking feeling in my stomach, and I already know the answer before she moves her foot and we both look down to see tails staring back up at us.

"The fox is called Hurriyah," Reema smiles, but her face is still sad.

"Fine." I roll my eyes. "Hirryayeah it is then, but I get to name the cubs, alright? All of them."

Reema's eyes narrow and she thinks for a minute, staring at the foxes that are watching us from behind the bin shed.

"Three of them," she says at last. "I will name the biggest one."

I want to argue about it, but I don't have any fight left in me. I'm too sad now the wee one is gone. "OK, but don't go calling her anything weird and hard to say like Hurrayeahyah, OK?"

"*Hur–ri–yah*," Reema says slowly, looking like she's ready to hit me if I get it wrong one more time.

"Right," I say quickly, "Hur–ri–yah. What does it mean again?"

"Freedom. Our fox is called Freedom."

The Fox

A cry on the wind. I stir and sit listening,
Hoping the sound is my little one, Five.
The call comes again and I close my eyes, heart-sick.
It is not my youngest, he will not return.

The rest remain sleeping, they grow with each sunrise,
Exploring the small-box and garden beyond.
They play in the open, tumbling and growling.
They will not stay hidden; I watch them, afraid.

The beasts in their box-den will soon find our hideout.
This place is not safe, so it cannot be home.
But I struggle to stand, and limp on my weak leg.
We must stay for now, though I long to be gone.

We cannot run free.
Not yet, not yet.
No, we cannot run free.
Not yet.

18

Reema

"What you still wearing that thing on your head for? You having a permanent bad hair day or something?"

"My dad says everyone who wears those things is a terrorist."

"You shouldn't wear that in this country. We believe in freedom, not like those countries where women have to wear black bin bags all the time."

"Take it off."

One of the boys snatches my *hijab* from my head before I can stop him and goes running off across the playground with it. The other boys follow, laughing and throwing it to each other. I chase after them, pleading with them to stop, but it just makes them laugh harder. I know why they are picking on me today. It is not because I am from another country and wear a headscarf, it is because I did better than them in the maths test this morning, and they do not like it. Andy always comes first, and he hated being beaten by a girl, especially one who still struggles to read and speak English like I do.

"Please give it back," I beg. "You will tear it!"

The faded silk is fragile now, just like all of us who survived the war. I cannot bear to see it torn to pieces in the careless hands of boys who have only ever known peace and comfort.

"Hey look, it's falling to bits!" Andy tugs on a loose thread and the end of the scarf starts to unravel, slowly at first and then faster as his friends cheer him on. It is as though he is cutting the last ties I have to my lost brother with every row of silk he pulls apart.

"Please stop!" I am crying now, my hands shaking as I reach for the scarf before he can destroy it beyond repair. "Please! It is my… my…" I cannot find the words to describe to these boys what this scarf means to me, and they laugh harder at my failed attempts at English.

"Oof!"

Suddenly all of the laughter stops. Andy is pinned up against the wall by a strong hand.

"Give. It. Back."

Caylin's eyes are so narrow they are like tiny pinpricks of menace that bore right through Andy's skull and burn into his brain.

"Now!"

She clenches her fist, and Andy whimpers and flings the scarf in my direction. I catch it before it can fall on the ground, bundling it up carefully and hugging it to my chest.

"Do that again and I'll beat the lot of you into jelly and eat you for lunch, got it?"

Despite my tears I notice that Caylin is very careful to avoid using the letter 's' when she speaks to anyone else in school.

She has to think hard before she says anything to make sure there are no sounds that will trip her, and her words come out slowly and carefully, as though they have been rehearsed in her head. This is what makes people think she is stupid, but I know now it is not true. She is not stupid, but she is half-wild, like Hurriyah, and will bite if you try to get too close.

It has been ages since we buried the smallest cub and agreed to share the feeding of the foxes, and we have barely spoken since. I am not sure yet if she can be my friend.

"You OK?" she asks as the boys run off, calling names over their shoulders and pretending they were not scared away by a girl. They will get their revenge by laughing at Caylin when Mrs Gibb makes her read aloud in class this afternoon, but she is clearly willing to risk this to help me.

Maybe we can be friends after all.

"Yes," I sniff, "it is not too bad. I can fix it." I wrap my *hijab* back round my head and tie the ends in a knot to stop them fraying any further until Mama can sew them back into place for me.

"Why do you wear it anyway?" Caylin asks. "Is it the law in your country or something?"

"Of course not! It is just … It is so hard to explain."

Instead of shrugging and walking away, Caylin sits down on one of the playground benches and waits.

I sit down beside her and fold my hands in my lap, playing with my fingers and searching for the words I will need. I am not used to telling my story. At home we barely speak of Jamal. It hurts too much to even mention his name.

"Before the war," I start slowly, "my brother... he buys it for me."

"Your brother?" Caylin looks surprised. "I didn't know you had a brother. Where is he? Oh..." She sees how pale my lips have become and stops short, afraid I will cry if she says any more. But I want to talk about Jamal. I am tired of never speaking his name in case I upset Mama and Baba.

"Jamal is my best friend," I tell her. "I have... other friends – Haya and Dilber and Lillian. I miss them also. But Jamal... he knows me best of all."

Caylin nods, her eyes sad. It seems to me she understands what it is to lose someone precious, but she does not tell me who. Instead she asks, "What was it like? The war? Was it really scary?"

"Yes. Scary, but also... how do you say it? Very... boring."

"Boring?" Caylin thinks I have chosen the wrong word, but I am certain it is the right one.

"The bombs, the guns, the soldiers... they are all scary. But for many days, there is nothing to do. No more work for Baba. No more school. We stay in the house, every day. We watch my movies, again and again. We must not go out. Too... danjeris? Then more fighting. Water and... eleksisity? They are all cut... no more movies. Then no more food. We are so hungry. Just crackers and rice."

There is a flash of understanding in Caylin's eyes. Somehow, even in this country of peace and plenty, she has tasted the hunger too. I lean forward, eager now to share more.

"Bombs come every day, and guns... fighting... everywhere. Baba says we must run. He goes to find... a safe road...

128

to Lebanon. You hear of the country Lebanon? But in Hama city… he is hurt. Gas bomb. He is… broken."

It is not the right word. Yet somehow it *is* the right word for Baba and the damage the nerve gas did to his big, strong body.

"Jamal says we must go… norf?"

"North."

"Yes, north, to the… safe camps… in Turkey. But Baba is too sick. He cannot walk. One night the bombs are so bad, our house… it is… broken."

That word again. The word that describes everything the war did to my country, my home, my family.

"And Jamal?" Caylin asks softly, as if she is afraid I will also break if she speaks too loud. "The bombs, did he…?"

I shake my head. "Not the bombs. When we run from Syria, Jamal… he is lost."

Caylin does not understand. And so for the very first time, I tell someone in this new country what happened the night we lost Jamal. The words hurt me so much I nearly choke on them as I force them out one by one.

"We run. We take nothing… no bags… no clothes… we can only carry Baba between us. But we cannot… carry Baba all the way," I say, searching for the words to describe that awful journey. "It is too far… the road… too long. A man in a truck… he says he will give us… a… what? A ride? But it is so full. No room. Just Baba and little Sara, he says. Mama begs and begs. We are so small and thin, she says… so hungry. Please let us come too. So the man says yes… But not Jamal. Jamal is too big, the man says… Jamal must walk."

I ball my hands into fists and try to hold on tight to the pain so it will not tear me to pieces.

"We wait and wait… at the camp. Days. Weeks. Months. No Jamal. He does not come. No one sees him. No one knows… if he is alive."

I swallow hard, my throat raw with the effort of holding back tears.

"I have nothing of… of my brother left now… No picture. No. Just this." I stroke the silk of my headscarf, trying to bury the guilt that has been eating me up from the inside ever since that night on the road.

"I am weak," I say, my voice breaking. "I should stay and walk with Jamal. But I am tired and scared… and selfish? Yes, selfish. I want to ride in the truck to the camp. So I leave Jamal behind… with the bombs and guns and fighting."

All the guilt comes flooding out, and with it the tears that I have been holding back for so long.

I left my brother alone on the road because I was too scared to let go of Mama's hand.

I am a selfish coward.

It is my fault Jamal is gone.

19
Caylin

Reema's crying again and it's making me feel really bad.

"It's not true," I try to tell her, "and you haven't just got a headscarf, you've got lots of good memories to remind you of your brother, don't you?"

That's what people used to say when Grandad died. It didn't help me feel any better, and it certainly didn't help Mum, but maybe it'll help Reema. It's worth a shot anyhow.

"Don't think about all the bad times, think about something good. What's the best thing you remember about your brother?"

Reema thinks for a minute, then her eyes light up through her tears.

"Ice cream!" she smiles. "In summer when the sun is shining, Jamal comes for me after school. Baba says to go straight home, but we stop at the café and he buys me ice cream with the money from his weekend job. It is our secret."

"That's a bit like my grandad," I grin. "I used to go to his house after school, and he'd give me money for the van and I'd buy ice cream and eat it on his back steps while he was making dinner. Mum never let me have ice cream before dinner, but Grandad always said it didn't matter to my stomach whether I had pudding first or last. He was good that way, my grandad."

I glance over to see that Reema's frowning again, struggling to understand what I'm saying. I try not to feel disappointed, but it's been so long since I've had anyone to talk to about Grandad that it's frustrating she can't keep up. It's just typical that the only person I can trust with my secrets is someone who barely understands a word I say.

"Money for the van?" Reema asks, looking confused.

"The ice cream van. You know, the one that comes round the houses playing a tune and selling sweets to the kids at home time?"

Reema's face is blank. At first it makes me think that talking to her about anything important to me is a waste of time. Then I have an idea. I know how to make her feel better about her brother, and how to make myself feel better about all the memories of Grandad swirling round my head and driving me half-mad with missing him.

I'm a genius.

"Right. We'll wait at the gate after school for your wee sister, then I'll show you what I'm talking about, OK?"

Reema nods, still looking a bit confused, and the bell rings for the end of break. Reema gets up and starts walking to where our class is lining up to go back in, but I head off a different way. I've seen a bunch of wee kids from the junior classes sneaking round to play by the bins outside the kitchen. They're not allowed near there because of the lorries that stop for delivery and pick-up, and that means they can't tell on me if I pinch their lunch money because I'll just tell on them back.

I jog round to the bins and grab the nearest wee kid by his hood. "You're Andy Lockwood's wee brother, aren't you? Give me your lunch money or I'll tell the head teacher on you. It's against the rules to play back here. You'll be in so much trouble you'll never be allowed out at break again."

The wee boy's face goes white with fright and he digs his hand straight into his pocket and pulls out a bunch of coins. I swipe them off him and put them in my own pocket, making sure the other kids don't run away before I've had a chance to collect a donation for the Caylin Todd financial fund from them too.

I don't worry about my lisp when I'm taking money off wee kids. They're too scared of my fists to laugh at my words. When I've got enough money I let them go, the coins jingling in my pocket as I hurry to catch up with my class line before it disappears back inside the school.

Reema throws me a questioning look when we sit back down at our table, but I don't explain, I just grin and say, "Later." I don't feel bad about stealing today. This time it isn't for me. This time it's to make Reema and her sister feel better. And nicking money off Andy's wee brother is just payback for Andy taking Reema's scarf and making her cry. I don't need to feel guilty. I won't let anything spoil the nice surprise I have planned.

I'm so impatient for it to be home time that the rest of the day seems to last forever.

Mrs Gibb drones on about the Roman times in Scotland

for so long I'm ready to chuck my pencil case at her to make her shut up. I pack my bag five minutes before the bell while she's still talking, but then Reema nudges me and I realise I should probably be paying attention instead of picking my nose and sticking the bogies on Andy's homework jotter.

"Miss Lindsey's asked me to remind you about the sports club starting up today at four o'clock," Mrs Gibb shouts over the noise of chairs being clattered under desks and schoolbags being zipped up. "It's open to anyone in primary six and seven, and later this term there'll be a chance to try out for the Glasgow schools athletics competition."

"You are going, yes?" Reema asks me. She looks eager.

I shake my head. "Nah," I shrug, "not interested." It's not true. I'd love more than anything to get a place at the big sports event, but I'm too scared to even try in case I disappoint Mum.

"But Caylin, you are so fast!" Reema tries to sweet-talk me into it. "You can win all the races, and—"

"Come on, let's go meet your sister," I interrupt. Mrs Gibb is coming towards me and I know she's going to remind me that she wants to talk with Mum about my behaviour and how I'm going to totally fail at high school if I don't pull my finger out and blahblahblah.

I'm too fast for her. I grab Reema by the arm and run out of the door before Mrs Gibb can call me back.

We meet Reema's wee sister at the school gate and I hurry them down the road, following the out-of-tune jingles coming from the ice cream van's loudspeaker.

"Hear that?" I tell them. "That's the van coming round. You

can get sweets and drinks from it, but today we're going to get something better."

It's a perfect May afternoon, and the sun is shining so hard it'll do itself an injury if it's not careful. That's what my Grandad always used to say when the weather was nice. The blue sky and the chimes of the van make me miss him so much I can barely breathe past the lump in my throat as I wait at the back of the queue. The coins in my pocket feel heavy, but I won't feel guilty, I won't.

Not today.

"Oh! Ice cream!"

Reema finally figures out what we're doing here when she sees a boy eating a cone with a big Flake stuck in it. Her face lights up as bright as the sun and I'm almost dazzled by her smile. Her little sister is nearly dancing in delight when we reach the front of the queue and I hand them a cone each. I've only got money for three wee ones without the Flakes, but it's enough to make Reema happy.

For the first time since the fox cub died, I feel happy too.

We stand by the side of the road, leaning up against the park railings and licking our ice creams as we watch the birds circling overhead, waiting for scraps. The sun shines down and tickles our skin until I'm so warm and my tongue's so cold I can't decide which one feels best.

Everything is perfect, right up until the moment Reema suddenly stops licking her ice cream and gives me a hard stare.

"Caylin," she asks, a frown knitting her eyebrows up into a big black tangle, "where did you get the money?"

"It's my pocket money," I shrug, trying to sound innocent.

"No. You do not get pocket money."

I don't think she even knows what pocket money is. She just knows that I'm lying.

"My mum gave it to me," I try again. "Don't worry about it."

But Reema *is* worrying about it. She isn't going to let it drop, and her suspicious eyes are making me nervous.

"She stole it from David Lockwood in my class," Sara butts in, all excited and proud of herself for having a secret her big sister doesn't know about. She's proud of her English too. She's only been here a couple of months and it's way better than Reema's already. "She beat him behind the school and stole his money. Kevin and Leanne's too. They told me in art class. David wants to tell the teacher, but Leanne says if they tell then Caylin will kill them. Do you kill people Caylin?"

Sara looks up at me, all innocent curiosity and vanilla-ice-cream chin.

"You *steal* it?" Reema cries. "*Caylin*! Stealing is *haram*! It is forbidden! It is *wrong*!"

"But—" Before I can tell her I only did it to make her feel better about her brother, she's snatched the cone out of Sara's hand and thrust them both back at me. Sara protests, but Reema grabs her by the arm, marching her down the road and leaving me standing there clutching three cones that melt slowly over my fingers and drip onto the ground.

I drop them on the concrete and stomp on them angrily, watching them turn into sad milky puddles. The birds can have them now. I don't want them. The ice cream in my stomach is making me feel sick. All I wanted to do was cheer Reema up and remind her of the good times she had with her brother. I guess I wanted to remember the good times I had with Grandad too, but all that's spoiled now.

I thought maybe Reema could be my friend, but I was wrong. I'm too bad to deserve any friends.

20
Reema

I should not be eating ice cream this month anyway. It is the first week of Ramadan, but only Mama is fasting each day from sunrise to sundown. Baba says it does not matter much any more: our family spent so long going hungry in the war that we have fasted a lifetime of holy months already.

I hate to hear him talk as though he has lost his faith.

Mama will not let me join her in the fast, even though Jamal started fasting for just a few days from the age of ten. She does not want me to suffer from hunger again, but she cannot protect me from the memories.

They come flooding back, and I am no longer in Glasgow.

I am walking alone through the streets of Aleppo, clutching a small bowl of rice stew to my chest as though it is full of precious diamonds. I am so afraid that my legs are shaking, but it is not just the snipers on the rooftops I fear. Sara has been coughing so hard all day I am scared her little body will break.

Mama did not want me to go to Aunt Amira's house to ask for food, but she knows without it Sara will not get better. "Run straight there and back," Mama said, holding my hand so tight

138

I thought she would not let go. She wanted to wait for Baba and Jamal, but they are tramping through the deserted *souks* in search of food, begging for scraps from the few traders who remain. They will not be back till after dark.

It is up to me to save my little sister. I must not fail.

I am just crossing the deserted square when it happens.

I am looking up, keeping my eyes on the windows of bombed-out houses and peering into the shadows of crumbling walls and alleyways to watch out for snipers. I do not see them coming. There are four of them – thin, desperate-looking young men who appear from the ruins of a shop like a pack of wolves on the hunt.

When they see my bowl they close in from all sides, their eyes wide with longing. If there had been no war and my legs were not weak from hunger, I would have run. I am the White Gazelle, and I am fast. But I am not fast today.

"Please!" I beg when they snatch my bowl and begin fighting over it. "It is all my family has!"

But they do not listen. They are mad with hunger, and push me aside so hard I fall in the gutter. By the time I pick myself up, the bowl is empty and the men are gone.

I am bruised and bloody from my fall, but knowing that I have let my little sister down and that she will go hungry tonight hurts most of all.

"Reema, stop! You are hurting me!"

I wake from my daydream and slow down, realising I have been pulling Sara along the road by the arm so hard the sleeve of her coat has ripped.

"I am sorry Sara, I just wanted to protect you."

"From what?" Sara glowers at me and rubs her arm.

From all the bad memories of war that have followed us here, I want to say. *From bullies like Caylin who steal from small children like you so she can buy ice cream. From everything that might hurt you, little sister.*

Instead I say, "That ice cream was bought with stolen money. You know that stealing is *haram* Sara. This is Ramadan, when we should remember all the people in the world who are hungry and be grateful for what we have. We should not be taking things from other people, it is wrong."

But Sara is too young to care about Ramadan. All she cares about is the big hole I have put in her only coat.

"You have spoiled it!" she cries. "I will tell Mama!"

She races on ahead of me, up the street and down the path to our apartment building. I could chase her, but today I am not in the mood for running.

When we get home Mama is not in the mood to listen to Sara's stories either.

"Where have you been?" she demands as soon as we come through the door. "I have been waiting for ages and we are already half an hour late for our English class."

I know this is an exaggeration. Our taxi is not even outside yet. I do not say this to Mama though. Her face looks washed out, and her eyes shimmer with uncried tears. It is not just because she is fasting, it is because she has been arguing with Baba about Jamal again.

"Is Baba coming to class with us?" Sara asks, forgetting about her coat for a moment when she sees Mama has left a plate of biscuits on the table for us. She is too young to know that this is the worst question to ask Mama right now. Baba is asleep in his room, exhausted after their argument, and he will probably stay there until long after sundown. Mama's lip trembles for a moment, but then she pulls herself together and her face is calm again.

"No, he is tired and needs to rest. We will go together, the three of us."

Our family used to be five. Now we are only three.

I feel awful when I have to tell her that I am leaving her as well.

"Mama, I am sorry, but I am going back to school in a little while. Our gym teacher Miss Lindsey is starting an after-school sports club and I promised her I would join. It is the first meeting today."

Mama does not look like she is listening to me. She is busy getting her coat and putting her English notebook in her bag for class.

"Not today, Reema. You have English lessons this afternoon."

"I speak English all day in school, I do not need extra lessons!" I lie. I do not speak English much in school. No one ever talks to me except the teachers and sometimes Caylin, and she will probably never speak to me again after I gave back her stolen ice cream.

"You will go to the English class with me and your sister, Reema, no arguments," Mama snaps.

I ball my hands up into fists and shout back, "No, I will not!"

In the silence that follows, I realise I sound a lot like Caylin. Maybe spending time with her has made me half-wild too.

Mama stares at me, first in surprise, and then in sorrow. She knows I would not have spoken to Baba like that. We both do.

"Very well, there is no time to talk about it now. We will discuss it tonight with your father."

Mama does not look at me again while she bundles Sara out of the door and closes it behind her. I can hear Sara's high-pitched whines about the hole in her coat and the biscuits she has not had time to eat fading away down the corridor. I hear the slam of a car door and the sound of the taxi driving off down the street.

When they are gone I feel empty inside.

Four members of my family survived the war, but I feel like the fighting has divided us all.

That is why I must keep my family of foxes together. Maybe if I can keep them safe there is hope that my family will be united again one day too.

I go to the kitchen and start preparing a meal for Hurriyah and her cubs, my heart aching with sadness the whole time.

21
Caylin

"Come on Caylin, make an effort!" Miss Lindsey calls.

I glower at her and deliberately miss hitting the next ball she throws right at my bat so that I have to sit out.

Stupid sports club. I don't want to be here anyway.

I wanted to go and feed the foxes to make myself feel better about the ice cream disaster, but Reema got there first. I don't want to talk to her again for as long as I live. I thought I could watch TV with Mum instead, but that was all spoiled too.

When I got back upstairs Mum was in no mood for talking. She was fussing about in the kitchen, opening cupboards and banging about with pots and pans. There was something burning on the cooker and I had to open a window before I choked to death on the fumes of onions that had been fried to death.

"Brian's coming for dinner tonight, and he's bringing Johnny so you'll have some company. That's nice, isn't it?" Mum said in her super-bright voice, the one she uses to pretend something she knows I'll hate is actually a good thing – like when she gives me cough medicine or wipes a cut with antiseptic that stings

the living daylights out of me. Brian and Johnny coming over is way worse than cough medicine or skinned knees though, and no amount of listening to Mum's singsong voice was going to make me like it.

"*Why?*" I whined. "They're *always* here! I *never* get peace from them."

"That's not true!" Mum protested. "I hardly ever have guests, and you know Brian and I are getting on really well."

Despite you trying to break us up at every opportunity, I could hear her wanting to add under her breath.

"Well, I won't be here." I snatched my schoolbag and grabbed a T-shirt and pair of shorts from the pile of clothes Mum had folded neatly on the ironing board. "I'm going to Miss Lindsey's sports club today."

"Caylin, that's wonderful! Your gran and grandad would be so proud!"

She was so excited she forgot her bubbling pots and pans and followed me all the way downstairs to see me off.

I can still hear her happy voice echoing in my head as I sit here at the side of the playground watching the other kids finish their game of rounders. I feel so guilty it's like my stomach's got a big bowling ball in it weighing me down.

I'm not here to make Mum happy.

I'm here to avoid her stupid new boyfriend and his snot-nosed son.

"OK, break time!" Miss Lindsey calls when the last batter misses her swing. "Take five minutes to catch your breath and have a drink. We'll have a game of dodgeball next."

The other kids crowd round the picnic tables and pull out their chocolate bars and cans of juice. Reema follows them, hovering shyly at the back of the group, but there's no room for her and it's clear she's not welcome. She comes over to sit beside me instead. I shuffle to the end of the bench and stare at the ground.

The loud laughter and chatter from the picnic tables is making me feel so lonely I wish I'd just stayed at home and put up with Brian and Johnny.

I wish I had friends to talk to.

I wish I hadn't stolen that ice cream money and spoiled everything with Reema.

I wish I could think of something to say to her that would make everything alright again.

Reema's restless. She's shifting about on the bench, tapping her feet and drumming her fingers on her knees. She's feeling uncomfortable too. She's been trying really hard in Miss Lindsey's games, so she's way more sweaty than me. She lifts the edge of her T-shirt, frowns at it, then says something I never thought I'd hear her say in a million years.

"I need a shower. I am … pure … dead … bogging."

It's so funny to hear her using Glaswegian words that I burst out laughing.

"Do I say that right?" Reema asks shyly. She's not sure I'm laughing for the right reasons.

"Yeah, apart from your accent," I snort. "That's totally rubbish."
"Rubbish?"
"Yeah, you know – terrible."

"Oh." Reema's face falls, and I feel a bit bad. She was trying to make friends again and I ruined it. "It's OK," I tell her, "I'm rubbish at lots of things too."

"I am… rubbish… at speaking English," Reema says slowly, trying out the new word she's just learned.

"I bet you think lots of things here are rubbish compared to back home," I say quickly, trying to keep the conversation going.

"Yes. The weather is… rubbish. And the school dinners… are rubbish."

I grin at that. "They're worse than rubbish. The school dinners are minging!"

"School dinners are… minging?"

"And the custard's totally boufing." I mime throwing up onto my ratty old trainers.

Reema laughs too. "*Minging* school dinners… and *boufing* custard!" she repeats. I don't mind teaching her words now. She's realised she shouldn't copy my lisp.

"Come on," Miss Lindsey blows her whistle again, "up you get! We'll split you into two teams for dodgeball."

"Aw Miss!" one of the primary-six girls groans. "Can we not have five more minutes? I'm knackered."

Reema throws me a puzzled look. "Tired," I tell her. "Knackered means tired. Or sometimes worn out, like my trainers, look." I hold up one foot so she can see the sole that's starting to peel away from the rest of my shoe.

"Yes, our shoes are *knackered*," Reema agrees. "Mine too." Hers don't look as bad as mine, but they're clearly second-hand.

It must be awful losing everything you own and having to wear other people's stuff all the time. My clothes might be a bit grubby and old, but at least no one else has ever worn them.

"Lisa, Andy, you pick the teams. Quickly now, we don't have all day," Miss Lindsey calls.

It doesn't take long for the other kids to be sorted into teams and for Reema and me to be left standing on our own.

Andy doesn't want to pick either of us. No big surprise there. "It's an odd number," he tells Miss Lindsey. "One of them'll need to sit out."

"They can both join Lisa's team," Miss Lindsey frowns at him. "It's not the Olympics." She doesn't like people whining about fairness any more than she likes me not trying.

Lisa rolls her eyes so hard it looks like they're going to come popping out of her head, but she keeps her mouth shut.

"Come on," I mutter to Reema, "let's show them how rubbish and slow they are compared to us."

Reema gives me a secret smile and nods to show she's understood.

I haven't forgotten about the ice cream and I'm pretty sure she hasn't either, but we're talking to each other again and that's something. This time when the game starts, I don't fold my arms and trudge round the dodgeball court like I couldn't care less. This time I really try.

The balls come flying furiously at us, and Reema and I dodge every one. We're fast, faster than all the other kids who've laughed at us and refused to sit with us at lunch or play with us at break. Soon it's just me and Reema left, and even the balls Miss Lindsey

147

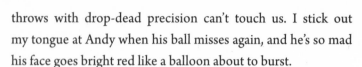

throws with drop-dead precision can't touch us. I stick out my tongue at Andy when his ball misses again, and he's so mad his face goes bright red like a balloon about to burst.

I could do this all day, but soon Miss Lindsey blows her whistle and spoils our fun. "Well done girls, that was great work! It's half five, so we'll have to pack up for today. I hope you enjoyed yourselves and will all come to the next session."

Andy's still glaring at us, so I hold my hand up to Reema and grin to show him he doesn't scare me. Reema looks puzzled for a moment, but then she smiles back and gives me the high-five I was waiting for.

"You are coming again next time?" she asks.

"Maybe," I shrug. This week was a one-off. I don't want Mum getting all excited about me joining the sports club and thinking I'm going to be a famous runner like Gran.

Even though Reema and me are talking again, we don't walk home together. I'm not ready to go back yet. Instead I go to the park and sit on the swings for an hour, waiting till it gets dark and I'm sure dinner's long over. By the time I walk down our street and see the lights in the flat windows, I start to worry that I might've stayed out a bit too late.

Mum's going to be mad at me.

But it's me who's mad when I see Brian's red car still parked on the pavement outside our block. As soon as I see the familiar furry dice dangling from the mirror the angry ache returns to gnaw at my belly.

I stomp my way upstairs, expecting Mum to be standing at the door ready to yell at me. I'm almost hoping she will. At least then

I'll know she's been thinking about me and not Brian. Instead, when I open the door I'm greeted by the sound of the TV blaring and laughter from the living room.

When I go in I see Brian on the couch with his arm round Mum, and Johnny sitting in her lap. There's a jumble of takeaway boxes on the coffee table and a pile of dirty plates. There's still a smokey pong coming from the kitchen where Mum's burnt pans are soaking in the sink. It's clear from all the Chinese food that Brian doesn't trust her to make a decent meal any more than I do.

"Caylin, I wondered where you'd got to." Brian turns round and smiles when he sees me. "Come and sit down and have dinner. I brought a takeaway so your mum didn't have to go to any bother. We left you most of the sweet-and-sour pork – your mum says it's your favourite."

How would Mum know? She hasn't got off her backside and bought me a Chinese meal in ages.

I'm torn between telling Brian that this isn't his house and it isn't up to him when I sit down and eat, and my mouth watering at the sweet smell coming from the boxes.

Then I see the pile of photo albums on the sofa.

Brian's got one open at a picture of Gran and Johnny's putting his greasy fingers all over it.

Mum sees my face going a funny colour and says quickly, "I was just telling them all about your gran, pet, and how you're a brilliant runner just like her. How did the sports club go? Are you going to run for your school this year in the competition?"

Her face is so eager I feel sick. It's bad enough Mum thinking

I'm going to make her proud with my running. I don't want her telling the whole world.

"I'm not a good runner, stop saying that! And Grandad wouldn't have wanted his pictures of Gran covered in minging chop-suey sauce!"

I snatch the albums up and stumble to my room, dropping one on the floor when I slam the door behind me. It falls open at a photo of Gran with a medal round her neck, her cheeks glowing from winning a big race. It's almost like the picture's laughing at me, reminding me what a total failure I am compared to her.

I throw myself down on my bed and pull my pillow over my head, trying to block out the sound of the TV and the laughter coming from the living room. It was bad enough when Brian was just taking up all of Mum's attention. Now he's practically moved in with us and he's brought his dumb kid with him too. Mum can pretend everything's fine again if she wants, but I'm not playing along this time.

I'm not going to pretend we're one big happy family now, no way.

The Fox

Moonbeams glow and night comes calling,
Soon I will rise and steal through the dark.
Not soft as a whisper, but limp-legged, hobbling.
 I am still broken, afraid of the pain.

  But I am a hunter, a digger of secrets,
   A reaper of field mice, a thief in the night.
   This now is not me, for I am the wildness.
   I dance in the shadows and run with the wind.

  Here not a hunter, but merely a beggar,
  Waiting for others to bring me my meat.
 This is no life for my young ones to learn from,
  Hiding and cowering, afraid to be seen.

  If I could leave, then I would escape now,
   Run far from the world of the two-legged beasts.
    The time will come soon when my leg will be mended –
     Straighter and stronger – and then we will run.

     The time will come soon,
     We will run, we will run.
     Yes, the time will come soon.
     We will *run*.

22

Reema

"Reema, this is the last time I will allow you to play games at that silly sports club instead of attending your English lessons!" Mama snaps as she marches to the door with Sara.

"But Mama, they are not silly games, running is—"

"Learning English is more important than playing!" Mama interrupts before I can explain. "Your father cannot work now and I have only a high-school education. We have lost everything. Our family will never save enough money to buy a house of our own here if you and Sara do not go to university and get good jobs."

Mama does not say that this is what Jamal would have done. She does not need to. His unspoken name hangs in the silence between us when she closes the door and walks to the taxi with Sara.

I am too upset after the argument to go to the sports club today. Instead I sit on the sofa with the Quran the mosque gave us, searching for the peace to calm my aching heart. I want to be a good daughter, a good sister, a good student. But more than anything I want to be a fast runner. Can I not be all of those things at the same time?

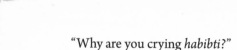

"Why are you crying *habibti?*"

I am so wrapped up in my own thoughts I do not hear Baba's footsteps on the carpet. He is getting better at walking with his crutches, but moving around still causes him pain. He eases himself down beside me and puts his arm around me like he used to when I was little. He has not done this in a very long time. When he reaches a shaky hand out to brush away my tears I know he is on my side.

"I am not Jamal!" I sniff, saying his name even though I know I should not. "I am never going to be as clever as him. But I can run Baba, I can run! The sports club is not just about playing games. If I train I could be an athlete, like the ones who compete in the Olympics!"

I know it is a silly dream, but Baba does not tell me so the way Mama would. He just gives me a sad smile and says, "Perhaps you could, Little Gazelle."

It is what Jamal always called me. I miss my big brother so much. We all do.

We are all searching for something to fill the hole he has left in our family. I have my running, Sara has her friends, and Mama has her English classes and her women's group at the mosque. Only Baba has nothing to keep his mind from the loss.

"Baba, will you read to me?" I offer the open Quran to him.

Baba is about to shake his head and get back up, but I will not let go of his hand.

"Please Baba? There is only one week of Ramadan left. Before the war you used to read to us every evening for the

154

whole month of Ramadan – do you remember? We would sit round the table at night, and Sara would be on Mama's knee, and Jamal would sometimes recite along with you to prove he had learned the verses, and I would fidget and fidget because I was not good at sitting still, and—"

I choke on the lump of memories in my throat.

"Peace *habibti*, there is no need to cry again. What are you reading?"

I pass him the book and he holds it in his trembling hands as though it is the most precious, fragile thing on earth. I thought he did not care about our religion any more, but when I see the way his fingers stroke the pages and hear the emotion in his voice as he reads, I realise it is because he cares too much.

I lay my head on his shoulder, the rough hair on his neck tickling my nose as I breathe in the familiar Baba smell. Baba's big body is thin now, and the once-strong arms feel bony as he holds me close, but this is still my father just the same. If I had really looked, I would have seen that the man I thought I had lost was right here beside me all along.

I close my eyes and listen as he recites, his voice becoming stronger with every page, each word sung out in prayer until he reaches the passage I have been waiting to hear.

"*Do you think that you will enter paradise without such trials as came to those who passed away before you? They experienced suffering and adversity and were so shaken in spirit that even the Prophet and the faithful who were with him cried, 'When will Allah's help come?' Ah, verily the help of Allah is near.*"

Baba stops reading and scratches his face, pretending he has an itch. But I know he is really brushing away a tear.

"Do you understand what that passage is about, *habibti*?"

"Yes Baba. It is about hope."

I know it is, because I have learned the verse by heart. It is the one I used to recite over and over to Sara when we were wrapped in a blanket sheltering under Mama and Baba's big bed when the bombers passed overhead.

"Then do not lose hope, Reema." Baba closes the Quran and places it carefully back on the shelf. "If you want to run instead of sitting in class, then you run. I cannot run any more. You must run for both of us."

Baba gets up stiffly and limps back to his room before I can tell him that he must not lose hope either.

I am about to go and prepare some food for the foxes to cheer myself up, when I hear a soft knock on the door.

When I open it I see Caylin standing in the hall holding a large box.

"Oh!" She blinks, surprised to see me. "I thought you'd all be out. My mum sent me down with this – it's some of my grandad's things that she doesn't need any more." She follows me into the living room, setting the box down reluctantly on the table.

"Thank you," I smile, even though we already have more donated plates and blankets than we will ever need. "It is very kind of you."

"Yeah, well, it wasn't my idea," Caylin mutters. It is clear she does not want to part with them. Maybe this is her way of apologising for buying me ice cream with stolen money.

"If they are special you do not need to—" I begin, but Caylin shakes her head.

"It's fine. I brought these for Sara. I'm a bit big for them now, so I thought she'd like to play with them."

She pulls a bag from the box and opens it, showing me the toy horses inside.

"Oh! Yes, Sara loves toys! We can put them in our room for a nice surprise when she is coming home."

Caylin likes the sound of that.

I show her the room I share with my little sister, and we have fun arranging all the horses on the windowsill and combing their long hair. Mama put up heavy net curtains so the nosey neighbours cannot not spy on us when they are hanging out their washing, but when we lift them up we can see one of the little foxes running across the garden.

"Someone will see them," I frown. "They are not safe here. Maybe we can take them somewhere else, somewhere quiet."

"No way!" Caylin says so loud I am afraid she will wake Baba. "This is their home! Anyway, it's illegal to move foxes to another place, they might starve or get attacked by other foxes. I saw it on a nature programme."

"Ill-eegil?" I do not understand her.

"We can't do it, OK? They belong here."

I do not want to argue, so I ask instead, "Do you give them names yet, the three small foxes?"

"Yeah, that one's called Jack." She points at the tail disappearing behind the bin shed.

"What does it mean?"

Caylin rolls her eyes the way she does when she is impatient or she thinks I am being stupid. "It's just a name," she mutters. "Why does it have to mean something?"

Because names are important, I think. *Only unimportant things have names that mean nothing.* I do not say this out loud though. Instead I say, "And the one with... more white on his chest? What is he called?"

"Barney," Caylin says. It is another strange name I have not heard before.

"And the other one? With black... what do you say... pitches? No, patches. Black patches around her eyes. What is her name?"

"Amber."

At least that is a name I know, but I am not sure I will remember the other names that mean nothing.

Caylin sees that I am not impressed by her choice of names, and her eyes narrow the same way Hurriyah's do when she feels threatened.

"So what have you called the biggest cub?" she scowls. "Something funny I can't pronounce?"

"No, it is a good name," I smile, remembering the words I just read with Baba. "I call her Amal."

"Huh," Caylin mutters. "At least that's easier to say than Hurriyah."

It is easier to say, but Amal's name is every bit as important as her mother's. The names Caylin gave the three other cubs, they are just people's names. But the name I gave the strongest fox means something special.

It means 'Hope'.

23
Caylin

She thinks they're just stupid names, but they're not. All of them mean something special to me, but it's so hard to explain to Reema that I don't even try.

Amber was the name Mum was going to give me when I was born, but Gran talked her into calling me Caylin instead, after my great-grandmother. I sometimes wonder whether I would've turned out a completely different person if I'd had the other name. Would Amber Todd have been all the things that I'm not? Would she have been clever and popular and kind and good? Would she have been a fast runner just like Gran and won medals and made Mum proud?

I can't help feeling like a disappointment compared to the imaginary girl I was supposed to be.

Barney is Barney Rubble, from the *Flintstones* cartoon I used to watch at Grandad's every Saturday. He used to pretend he wasn't interested in my kids' TV shows, but as soon as Mum dropped me off he'd sit down and watch them with me and laugh his head off at all the lame jokes.

Jack is short for Applejack. I was mad about My Little Pony, and Grandad used to buy me a new one every Christmas and birthday. That's why there are so many on Reema's windowsill. I'm still not sure I should have given them away, but maybe Mum's right, maybe it's time.

"Sara will be so happy to see these," Reema smiles as she finishes plaiting the white hair on the Cotton Candy pony. "She misses her toys from home. Thank you for sharing."

"Yeah, well, I kept my favourite one," I admit, a bit embarrassed. I still keep my Applejack pony on my nightstand so I can hold it when I'm feeling sad about Grandad. Maybe Reema with her headscarf that reminds her of her brother would understand that, but I don't know if I'm ready to talk about it yet. "Shouldn't you be at the sports club just now?" I say to change the subject.

"Yes. So should you," she shoots straight back. "You must come back to the club too, Caylin. You are fast. You must run for our school in the competition, and we must beat the other schools."

I shrug, pretending this doesn't interest me. There's a big interschool sports meet held every summer, when Drumhill Primary competes against the other seven schools in the area. We never do very well. *Dumb-hill*, the other school kids call us. Maybe they're right. We're not much good at anything.

"You are fast, more fast than Lisa Barton or Zoe Weir," Reema says. "You can win the one hundred metres race, and the two hundred."

Reema doesn't admit that I'm faster than her over a short distance, but I know that's what she's saying, and it almost makes me smile. Then I remember I don't want anyone to know I can run. The other kids wouldn't cheer for me in a race the way they'd cheer for Lisa and Zoe. They'd only laugh. And what if I'm not any good compared to the runners from posh schools with proper sports training? The thought of Mum getting all excited about watching me race and then me letting her down by coming in last turns my stomach.

"Nah," I say carelessly, "it's not my thing."

"But you are so good!" Reema frowns. "Why do you not run? The sports… ah… trials? They are next week, and then Miss Lindsey picks our school team. You are on the team if you run, Caylin. You must be."

She makes it sound like an order rather than a suggestion. I'm about to tell her where Miss Lindsey can stick her sports team when Reema's little sister comes running into the room.

"Oh! My Little Pony!" Sara squeals with delight as soon as she sees the toys on the windowsill. "Just like the ones Jenny and Lauren have! Reema, where did you get them?"

"They are a present from Caylin," Reema says. "They are her favourite toys, so you must look after them, Sara."

Sara gives me a big hug, and I can feel my face turning red again. Mum and me had a blazing row before I agreed to give my old toys away. She was right though – it feels good to share.

"Let's play horse school. This is the teacher horse, and you have that horse Caylin, and Reema, your horse is just starting a new school, and…" Sara babbles away, ordering us about and arranging the horses on the carpet until we're all laughing at how bossy she is.

"She is worse than Mrs Gibb, yes?" Reema rolls her eyes at me.

"*Way* worse!" I agree. "She'd better not give us any My Little Pony homework to do."

Reema grins back at me, but when she sees the clock on the wall she jumps up, saying something to Sara in their language.

"What's up?" I ask.

"Nothing," Reema says in English. "It is our prayer time now. Come on Sara, we have to wash."

"But I want to play!" Sara whines, dragging her heels all the way to the bathroom.

I get up and start tidying the ponies away in their bag, but Reema says, "You do not have to leave, Caylin. You can stay."

"But isn't it kind of... private?" I ask.

"No. Anyone can watch our *salat*. At home, in Syria, people pray in schools, in shops, and even at the roadside."

When she comes back after washing she's carrying a big rug that she spreads on the floor. There's enough room for her and her wee sister, and they start chanting together, bending down on the rug in a smooth series of movements and standing up again, over and over.

At first I think it looks a bit silly, but after a while the words start to sound like music and the up-and-down motion as they bend down on the rug starts to feel soothing. It's a bit like when I used to sit in Grandad's kitchen while he was cooking, listening to the radio and watching the washing machine go round and round. No matter how bad a day I had in school, it always used to make me feel calm. At peace.

When Reema and Sara have finished they roll the rug up

again and Reema asks, "Do you think it is strange?" She's sort of looking at me out of the corner of her eye, and I realise this is a test. She's just showed me something really important to her and she wants to know if I'm going to take it seriously or make a joke of it.

I decide not to tell her about Grandad's washing machine. I don't think she'd like the comparison. Instead I say, "It was nice. Like music and dancing. I liked watching. Thanks for letting me stay."

Reema grins, and I know I've said the right thing.

But this isn't going to work. We can't be real friends.

Not unless I'm willing to show her something important too. She's told me all about her life and her brother and the war and her headscarf. Now she's even showed me her prayers. I haven't shared anything about myself with her. I didn't try very hard to tell her about Grandad, I just gave up when she didn't understand straight away.

If we're going to be friends, I'll have to try harder.

"Reema, are you and Sara free on Sunday?"

"Yes, I think so. Why?"

"I want to take you somewhere, somewhere special. Somewhere I've never taken anyone else before."

Reema smiles. She knows I'm starting to trust her at last.

24
Reema

"And you call this… *fishing?*" I pull the small net out of the water again and look inside to see if I have caught one of the tiny fish that swim near the surface of the canal.

Sara and Caylin's not-brother Johnny are much better at this than I am. They have already filled two jars with the little creatures and now they are sitting on the bank examining them in the sunlight, arguing about who has caught the biggest. I have only three in my jar because I am too busy listening to Caylin's stories of her grandfather to pay much attention to my net.

"So, then there was this time that a policeman came along, and me and Grandad had to sit on his fishing pole with our jackets over it because we didn't have a permit. It nearly dug a big hole in my bum, that pole, but I was laughing so hard I didn't notice till after. Anyway, when Grandad tried to use his rod again there was a big bend in it, and when he cast the line out it went sideways. He had to stand at a funny angle every time he went fishing after that, till Mum felt sorry for him and bought him another rod for Christmas."

Caylin is laughing so hard there are tears in her eyes. I do not understand all of her words, but I am laughing too. I have never heard her speak so much before. It is almost as though she has forgotten she has a lisp today. She speaks much more clearly when she is relaxed, and I like the way her eyes light up when she smiles.

"Look Caylin, I've got the biggest one!" Johnny runs over and shows Caylin his jar proudly, and she looks at the stickleback he is pointing out and nods her approval.

"Not bad, think you might be getting close to my record for the longest fish ever caught in this canal with that one."

"How big was your biggest one?" Johnny asks eagerly.

"This big!" Caylin holds her arms so wide the fish she is describing would be longer than Johnny himself. His eyes go wide for a moment, then he bursts out laughing and runs to show me his prize stickleback too. Caylin grins and starts pulling out sandwiches and cans of juice from the bag she has brought.

I am glad she is no longer angry that she had to bring Johnny too.

When we met her at the bottom of the stairs today she was so full of rage I could almost see smoke coming out of her ears. She barely said a word to us as we followed her to the canal, pulling Johnny so hard by the arm I was scared she would tug it right out of the socket. He did not complain though and carried the net on a long pole that Caylin thrust at him as though it was the most important job on earth.

Things did not improve until we were down by the

canal and Caylin was showing us how to dip the small net into the water and chase the tiny fish that scattered in all directions. Sara got the hang of it straight away and soon caught a stickleback for her jar, but Johnny is not very big and struggled to hold his pole and control the net when it was in the water.

At first Caylin ignored him, but after a while she got up to help, showing him the best way to hold the pole and how to scoop the net instead of just moving it sideways. When he finally caught his first fish she was grinning too, though she tried to hide it.

I think she likes showing the other children what to do for once. I think maybe it makes her feel important. From the way she talks about her grandfather, I think perhaps he used to make her feel like that too.

"So… how's the running going?" Caylin asks as we tuck into the picnic of sandwiches and crisps and soda. She says it casually, as though it has just popped into her head, but I know she has been thinking about it since I told her about the trials. She is a lot more interested in the competition than she pretends to be.

"It is good," I nod. "Zoe and Lisa both are fast. On Thursday Miss Lindsey is… picking runners… for the girls' team. Zoe and Lisa can run in the one hundred or two hundred metres race. They can maybe even win a medal."

I know that will get Caylin's attention. Those are her best distances. She will not like to think of those two other girls winning a prize that could be hers.

"What about you, what distance are you best at?" she asks.

"Miss Lindsey says if she picks me, I must run in the four hundred and eight hundred metres races," I tell her. "But she does not decide about the relay races yet. That… *depends*? Depends on who is picked for the team."

I glance sideways at Caylin. She is staring off across the water like she does not care, but she is also frowning and chewing her lip. I know she is thinking hard.

I do not want to drive her away with my questions, but like Baba with his wheelchair, sometimes Caylin needs to be pushed. "Are you running for the trials on Thursday?" I try to sound as unconcerned about it as she does.

Caylin frowns harder and then shrugs.

"Maybe," she says at last.

I smile, but I do not let her see.

We sit and watch the sunlight sparkling on the water until the rays turn from bright yellow to golden honey, and then I help Caylin gather up the little fishing nets and the remains of the picnic.

"Come on, pour those back in," Caylin tells Sara and Johnny when they beg to bring their jars home.

"But I want to keep them!" Johnny wails.

Instead of snapping at him, Caylin bends down and looks him in the eye. "Those fish all have a home of their own," she tells him. "Think how sad all the mum and dad fish will be if you go taking their kids away from them. They'll die in those wee jars Johnny, they're not your playthings. If you put them back then they'll still be there next time we come."

Johnny nods his understanding, and he and Sara pour all the jars of sticklebacks carefully back into the canal. I have a feeling those are not Caylin's words. I think she heard them from her grandfather when she was a small girl who wanted to bring her jar of fish home.

It is nice to see her sharing with other children, but I know she has something even more important to show them than the special places her grandfather used to take her. If she can be brave and show everyone how good she is at running, I think it will make her happy.

I used to think Caylin Todd did not deserve to be happy, but now I know I was wrong.

25
Caylin

I didn't want to take Johnny to my special place, but Mum made me because Brian was driving her to a job interview at a new hairdressers. I thought the kid would be a pain in the neck, but instead it turned out to be fun teaching him how to fish and telling him all the stories about monsters in the canal that Grandad used to tell me.

The sun is shining, Johnny is skipping back home holding my hand, and Reema and Sara are having a play fight with the fishing nets and getting big wet patches on their T-shirts.

I haven't had a day like this in a long, long time.

I thought coming here would make me sad, but I'm so happy I'd start singing if I didn't have a voice like a strangled cat. Maybe I've been wrong about a lot of things. Would it be so bad if I tried out for the athletics competition? Maybe Reema's right and I could be a runner after all. Maybe I *could* make Mum proud. Maybe—

"Caylin," Sara says suddenly, "Reema says you're a fast runner and you're going to be in the school team like her. Who's faster though, you or Reema?"

Reema shoots Sara a warning look, then gives me an apologetic smile. "We are good at different distances," she says quickly. "We are not running in the same races in the competition."

"Yes, but if you *are*," Sara insists in that annoying way wee kids do, "who will win?"

Reema's squirming with embarrassment and trying to shut her up, but nothing can ruin this day for me now.

"Why don't we see?" I grin. "You up for a race, Reema? Last one back to the flats gets to wash out the fishing nets."

She looks wary at first, but then she sees I'm just having a laugh and I don't really care who wins. We're at the top of the street and there's only a short row of houses to run past anyway, so it's not like it'll be a proper race. We hand the nets and bags to Johnny and Sara and get them to give us a countdown, giggling and jostling each other at the starting line to get away first. We don't try hard though. This is just a bit of fun.

At least it is until Darren's dog comes running across the road and starts chasing us down the street.

It jumps up and tries to bite Reema's arm, and she screams and trips, falling onto the ground and scraping her hands. I don't have a fishing pole to hit it with and I don't know what to do when it snaps at her face. I want to kick it, but my knees are shaking and I'm too scared.

Before it can take a bite out of Reema's cheek, Darren steps out from behind a parked car and grabs the dog round the neck, putting its lead back on again. He isn't sorry it nearly hurt Reema. He's smiling, and I can see all the gaps in his teeth and smell the beer on his breath.

"Thought I told you your kind aren't welcome round here!" he snarls at Reema, just as mean as his dog. "Next time I won't hold Prince here back, next time I'll let him—"

"What the hell are you playing at?"

Brian comes running down the path from the flats and lifts Reema to her feet, stepping between us and Darren, and shielding us from the slobbering dog.

Brian's a big guy, and Darren looks like a skinny wee thing standing next to him.

"Get that dog out of here before I call animal control and have it put down!" Brian yells. "If I see you hanging round this street again, I'll have the police on you, understand?"

Darren's face goes white and he backs off, hurrying down the road dragging his monster dog behind him. He's probably still on probation and scared of getting sent back to jail. Or maybe he's just a big coward who can't stand up to anyone who isn't a twelve-year-old girl.

"Are you OK pet?" Brian's rubbing the dirt from Reema's hands and making sure they're not cut too badly, but he's looking at me. We both nod, and Johnny and Sara come running up, struggling under the weight of the fishing rods and jam jars. I take the rods from them so Sara can hug Reema and Brian can pick Johnny up and stop him crying. His wee lip's trembling in fright and I almost feel like hugging him too.

I thought nothing could ruin this day for me.

I was wrong.

When we get back up the wheelchair ramp and into our close there's another nasty shock waiting for us. Someone's taken a can of spray paint to the walls and written in big, badly spelt words right next to Reema's front door:

TERERISTS GO HOME!

Her mum's standing there crying, and my mum's got an arm round her shoulder, and Reema's dad is shaking so badly Brian has to put Johnny down so he can grab him under the arms to stop him falling.

When Reema sees the words on the wall she starts crying too.

I want to scrub away the graffiti, but Brian says we have to wait for the police to see it first. While he's busy calling them we all go into Reema's flat. Her dad takes some medicine and goes to lie down, and Mum helps Mrs Haddad make tea in the kitchen.

"Don't worry." I sit down on the sofa next to Reema and her wee sister, giving Reema's arm a squeeze the way I saw Mum do with Mrs Haddad. "We're going to find whoever did this so we can make them pay."

Reema's stopped crying, and she's rocking Sara on her knee and talking softly to her in Arabic. When she turns to look at me her face is full of fire, but her eyes aren't angry, they're just determined.

"No Caylin," she says firmly, "we are going to find out who did this so we can *forgive* them."

I blink. Sometimes I just do not get her at all.

26
Reema

"What's *she* doing here?" Zoe mutters to the other girls in the changing room. "She doesn't belong here. She gave up after the first day. There's no way Miss Lindsey'll pick someone who doesn't make an effort."

"She's not going to try out for the team is she?" Lisa smirks. "I've seen three-legged dogs that can run faster than her."

They are not talking about me. They are talking about Caylin.

Caylin glowers at them as she pulls on her old tracksuit and battered trainers. I can tell she wants to say something mean right back, but she is afraid of drawing more attention to herself and of Lisa making fun of her lisp. She is not so brave facing other children when they are in groups.

The girls nudge each other and giggle as they hurry off to the playground. Our school does not have a proper sports field, or even a football pitch. I do not mind. I am used to running through the streets of Aleppo. Concrete is what I know best.

"Are you ready?" I ask Caylin. I am not really asking about her gym clothes.

"Dunno," Caylin shrugs without getting up from the bench. "Look, maybe this isn't such a great—"

"Caylin, we have talked about this." I catch hold of her arm and haul her to her feet. "You are the fastest runner in this school. Today you must prove it. Come, it is time to go."

I know she does not like to be stared at by the other children, but if she is going to use her gift then she must get used to people watching her run. I will not let her back out of this today.

She follows me unwillingly to the playground where Miss Lindsey is giving instructions to the large group of girls who have shown up for the trials. The boys raced yesterday and their team has already been picked. Today it is our turn.

"I'm going to time each of you individually over one hundred metres, then the eight fastest will run a race. The top four will make the team," Miss Lindsey tells us. "We'll repeat the individual trials over four hundred metres with a deciding race, and again I'll choose the top four. I don't want to hear any complaints if the same four are chosen both times!" she warns.

She is saying this because she thinks she already knows that Zoe, Lisa and I will win both races, along with another girl in our class called Pamela. She does not yet know about Caylin.

I smile secretly to myself as we line up in a row at the starting mark ready for our individual time trial. I cannot wait to see the other girls congratulate Caylin on how fast at running she is.

Zoe from the year below us goes first. She is smaller than the girls from our class, but her legs seem to work at twice the speed. She is a little faster than Lisa, who runs second, but not much. A few other girls run and then it is my turn. This is not my best distance, but I am determined to make the team, and I am ready.

When Miss Lindsey blows her whistle for me to start I throw myself forward and race for the finish line. I try to pretend that Jamal is right behind me, laughing and saying that if I do not speed up he will trip over my heels, but I feel naked without the headscarf Miss Lindsey does not like me to wear for sports. I cross the chalk mark on the ground and Miss Lindsey stops her watch and scribbles a number, but I am not pleased with my performance.

I know if Jamal had really been running with me I would have done better.

I swallow hard and push thoughts of my brother away, stepping aside to watch Caylin run. Everyone is watching her, whispering and giggling behind their hands. They are expecting her to fail.

When Miss Lindsey blows her whistle Caylin takes off so fast I can hear a gasp from the other girls. She does not run as though she has a proud big brother behind her, secretly urging her on and willing her to win. She runs as though she is being chased by Darren's big black dog, her eyes wild and her feet pounding the concrete in long strides.

It is not a pretty running style, but it works.

It works so well that Miss Lindsey looks shocked as she writes down Caylin's time on her clipboard. "Well done!" she says. "That was … unexpected."

I grin at Caylin, but she is not smiling yet. She has only won half the battle.

When the fastest eight line up to race I know I have to do better.

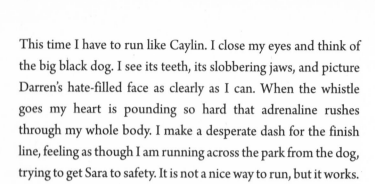

This time I have to run like Caylin. I close my eyes and think of the big black dog. I see its teeth, its slobbering jaws, and picture Darren's hate-filled face as clearly as I can. When the whistle goes my heart is pounding so hard that adrenaline rushes through my whole body. I make a desperate dash for the finish line, feeling as though I am running across the park from the dog, trying to get Sara to safety. It is not a nice way to run, but it works. I cross the line third. I look up, expecting to see Caylin ahead of me, but Zoe and Lisa have come in first. Then I look back and get a shock.

Caylin has not won the race.

She has not even finished.

She is getting up from the concrete where she has fallen, the skin on one knee scraped raw. There are tears glistening in her eyes, but they are not tears of pain and defeat. They are tears of anger.

"She pushed me!" Caylin yells, pointing at Zoe. "She shoved me and made me fall! It's not fair Miss Lindsey, it's not fair!"

"I didn't touch her!" Zoe says it so fast I know straight away she is lying. "I wasn't anywhere near her."

"First four across the line, that's what you said Miss Lindsey," Lisa chimes in, looking smug. "It was Zoe, then me, then Reema, and Pamela got fourth place. If Caylin's too clumsy to stay on her feet without falling she shouldn't be in the team anyway."

I hold my breath, waiting for Miss Lindsey's decision. The gym teacher does not like Caylin. Caylin never makes any effort in her class, and she has never shown any promise at running before. Miss Lindsey looks at her clipboard, her eyes checking the number she wrote down for Caylin's individual trial as though she cannot quite believe it.

"Can we run again?" I ask quickly, before she can decide Caylin's performance was just an accident. "Please? I am running with Caylin before, and she is really fast. Faster than me."

It's not strictly true, but it is not enough of a lie to make me feel guilty.

Miss Lindsey purses her lips, but then she nods. "OK, but we don't need to redo the whole race. Pamela, you came in fourth, so I'd like you to race Caylin to see who's fastest."

The other girls complain loudly, but Miss Lindsey has made up her mind.

When Caylin and Pamela line up behind the chalk mark my heart is pounding almost as hard as it was for my own race. The whistle goes, and I chant, *Do not fall! Do not fall!* over and over in my head so many times it sounds like a prayer. Caylin's leg is sore, but she is clearly too angry at the other girls to let it show. She comes roaring through the finish line like an angry bull, a clear three metres ahead of Pamela.

Zoe and Lisa glare at her, but there is no denying the truth now.

Caylin is fast. She deserves to be on the team.

The trials for the four hundred metres pass by in a blur. This is my best distance, and I find my rhythm quickly in my individual race, crossing the line in a time I know will not be beaten.

Caylin is still shaken by her fall though, and her legs are not steady. Her time is not good, and when the other girls have run she only scrapes into eighth place.

I know she has made the team for the one hundred metres relay race already, but it is not enough. On competition day I want her running with me in the four hundred metres relay too. This time I cannot help her though. It is up to her.

I glance across the starting line for the second race and see her looking back at me. Her eyes are determined. We nod at each other. Miss Lindsey's whistle goes and time collapses, standing still as our feet pound the ground, our arms pump the air and our lungs burn with effort.

When we cross the finish line and time starts again, I am first. I knew I would be.

We all look to Miss Lindsey. She calls out four names. The blood is pounding in my ears so loud I do not hear them. It is only when I see the disappointment in the faces of four of the girls, and the way Pamela's lip twists as she storms off, that I realise what has happened. Caylin will be running the second relay race with Zoe, Lisa and me after all.

Miss Lindsey congratulates us and tells us to make sure we are ready after school on Monday to start our training. When she walks back to the big group of girls waiting to try out for the jumping and throwing events I do not know whether to laugh with happiness or cry with relief.

Caylin also looks half-amazed and half-delighted, but her smile turns into a scowl when Zoe and Lisa walk past and Zoe snaps, "You don't belong in this team." She mutters something under her breath that sounds like 'thief', but I do not hear it clearly, so I cannot be sure.

"Why does Zoe hate you so much?" I ask when they are gone.

Caylin turns red and looks away. She has done something bad and she does not want to tell me.

"Whatever it is, you can apologise, you can make friends with her. You must Caylin, for the sake of the team."

Caylin rolls her eyes and rubs her aching leg. "Don't you get it, Reema?" she scowls. "We're never going to be a team. You and me are friends, and Zoe and Lisa are friends. It's us against them."

27
Caylin

I only got a second chance at the race yesterday because of Reema. She stood up for me when no one else would, and I won't ever forget it.

Mum and Brian and Johnny and me are at her place now for their end of Ramadan feast, and we're so full of food I think my stomach's going to burst. It was a bit awkward at first, as Reema's mum only speaks a wee bit of English and her dad doesn't speak any at all. But with Reema and Sara translating, and Brian making us all laugh with the feeble attempts at Arabic he kept looking up on his phone, dinner turned out to be a lot of fun.

Mum even ate the flatbread and dips without making a fuss about using her fingers, and I liked sitting round the table sharing food from the same plates. It was a proper family meal, and it felt good. Maybe next time Brian comes round with Johnny for dinner I'll sit and eat it with them instead of just shovelling something onto a plate and hiding in my room to eat alone.

"Try a pastry Caylin, you will like." Mrs Haddad hands another big bowl round, and I nearly groan at the thought of trying to cram more food in.

"Thanks Mrs Haddad, but I've had so much chicken casserole and fish and rice my belly's going to pop open and make a mess on your floor."

Sara bursts out laughing at the idea, so even though Mrs Haddad doesn't understand, she takes it as a compliment to her cooking. She puts one of her honey pastries on a wee plate and leaves it on the sofa beside me so I can eat it when I'm ready. I think I might have to wait another hundred years before I'm ever going to need to eat again.

"It must've taken your mum days to make all this food," I tell Reema. "Is this what you do every year?"

"We have not had an *Eid al-Fitr* celebration in years." She shakes her head. "This is our first in a long time."

"Oh yeah, of course."

Because of the war. I forgot. But just for tonight it looks like Reema and Sara and her parents have forgotten too. They're all looking happier than I've ever seen them, although Mrs Haddad and her husband sometimes glance to an empty chair in the corner. They might have forgotten the war for a few hours, but I guess they're never going to forget that their son's not here.

"Mama, do we get a gift this year?" Sara says eagerly in English. "I saw you wrapping something earlier – was it for me?"

It's funny how she automatically uses English now when I'm in the room. Her mother works out what she's saying and smiles, going to her bedroom and bringing back two parcels.

"Oh, are we meant to give presents?" I ask, a bit embarrassed. "Sorry, I didn't know."

"No, this is not like your Christmas," Reema smiles. "Our parents like to give us something new to wear on *Eid*, something useful."

Huh. I got a new coat and shoes last Christmas as Mum couldn't afford to buy them during the year, but I don't say this to Reema. I think she'd understand though, her family's been relying on handouts too. Maybe now that Mum's working again, this year will be different.

Johnny's a nosey wee brat and he 'helps' Sara open her present by ripping most of the paper off himself, but she doesn't mind as she's just as eager to see what's inside. She pulls out a fancy party dress and gives a squeal of delight, forgetting her English and chattering away in excited Arabic.

"She is always invited to birthday parties," Reema says. "She is very popular here with lots of friends. I think she will wear that dress many times this summer." Reema doesn't look jealous the way I would though, she just looks proud.

"What did you get?" I ask, tempted to help her pull off the shiny paper myself so I can see what's inside. Reema's way more patient than her sister, and she takes the time to turn over the gift tag and read what her mother's written there in Arabic. There's a line of messy English underneath that says, "To our White Gazelle, love Mama and Baba."

"White Gazelle? What's that?" I wonder.

"It is my name," she explains. "That is what the name Reema means."

I remember the names she's given the foxes and the way she keeps insisting that everything has to have an important meaning.

182

"Really? That's pretty good. I wish my name meant something."

"How do you know it does not?"

"Because…" I blink, realising I don't.

When Reema unwraps her parcel a piece of blue material falls out. At first I think it's just a really boring T-shirt, until Reema's smile lights up the whole room.

"*Eid Sa'id*, Reema," her mother says, and I know this means 'Happy Eid' because Reema's been making me practise saying it right all week. When Reema launches herself out of her chair to hug her mum, I pick up the bit of blue cloth. When I turn it over I see that it's a headscarf, but it's not like her green one. This one's made of the same material as our gym clothes so it won't flap about when she runs.

"It's a sports *hijab*," Sara tells me, trying it on before Reema can snatch it off her. "It's for Reema's running."

Reema's dad is grinning at her, and she gives him a big hug as well, careful not to squeeze too hard and hurt him. She told me her mum wasn't happy about her going to the sports club and missing English classes, so I guess her dad must've talked Mrs Haddad round. He's looking a lot happier tonight. I don't know whether it's because the drugs and physiotherapy he's been getting every week at the hospital are helping with his fits or because Brian was talking to him all through dinner with Sara's help about the jobs he could do here. Mr Haddad used to be a mechanic with his own big garage and lots of workers, and Brian says he knows some people who could give him a hand getting started doing repair work again part-time when he's better.

Brian's always helping people out like that. I don't know why I ever thought he was like all the other loser boyfriends Mum's had.

Mrs Haddad and Mum go back to the kitchen and make more tea, and I can hear them talking in really bad English about the athletics competition. Mum's so proud of me for making the team she hasn't stopped smiling since I came home from school yesterday. When she started her new job at the hairdressers today she told everyone that her Caylin's going to the inter-schools competition and they should come and see me run. She's invited half of Drumhill to watch already even though the competition Sunday isn't for over two weeks, the day after my twelfth birthday.

The thought of doing badly and disappointing her is making me feel so sick I nearly throw up all the food in my overstuffed belly.

"We go watch together," I hear Reema's mum saying. "We be… how you say? *Soccer moms?*"

Mum cackles so loud it's like a machine gun going off, but no one flinches except me. Thick as thieves those two are already. With Reema's translation help, Mum's even got Mrs Haddad all excited about the idea of starting a hairdressing course at college in the autumn.

Reema's admiring her new sports headscarf in the mirror, but I'm fiddling with the gift tag from her present. *White Gazelle*, I read again. What an awesome thing to be called. Can Reema be right about my name meaning something too?

"Hey Brian, can I borrow your phone for a minute?" I ask. Brian tosses it over and I check the internet, scrolling slowly through the search results until Reema comes over to ask what I'm looking at.

"I was just checking if my name means anything." I try to make it sound like I don't really care if it does or not. Reema's too smart to be fooled though, and she comes to sit down beside me when I find the right website.

"There!" she points. "CAYLIN. It means… 'lass'? What is a 'lass'?"

"It's just a Scottish word that means 'girl'. My grandad said it sometimes." I try not to sound disappointed, but 'girl' is a wee bit rubbish compared to 'White Gazelle'.

I'm about to put the phone down when Reema says, "And your other name?"

"I haven't got another name."

"Yes you do – Todd. What does that mean?"

"It's just a surname," I mutter, but I look it up anyway. When I see the search results my skin starts tingling and my heart beats so loud in excitement I'm pretty sure Mum and Mrs Haddad can hear it all the way from the kitchen.

"It means 'fox'!" Reema gasps. "Oh Caylin, you are the Fox Girl!"

For the rest of the night I feel like dancing with happiness.

There's only one thing that spoils this evening a bit, and that's Mrs Mitchell.

When we've helped clean up and said our goodbyes, Brian carries Johnny upstairs as the greedy wee grub's eaten himself to sleep, and Mum goes back up with them to get their jackets so they can go home. I hang around for a while talking to Reema

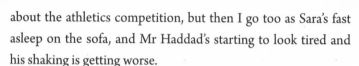

about the athletics competition, but then I go too as Sara's fast asleep on the sofa, and Mr Haddad's starting to look tired and his shaking is getting worse.

When the door closes and I'm out in the dark hall, I notice Mrs Mitchell's door is open. I don't know why that worries me. The nosey old bat likes to keep her door open a crack so she can hover round listening in to people's conversations and hear who's coming and going on the stairs. Tonight it makes me nervous though, and I tiptoe to the end of the close to check on the foxes just in case.

"Hello Caylin," she scowls. "What are you doing out this late?"

"I, er…" I could ask her the same thing, but she's a grown-up and she doesn't need an excuse.

"You're always out here with your wee friend," Mrs Mitchell says accusingly.

"We're just playing," I lie. This can't be about the bins again. Ever since Reema knocked over those bins and Mrs Mitchell started muttering about phoning the Council, we've been making sure the shed's in perfect condition. It's never been tidier. Mrs Mitchell can't have any reason to phone the Council now. Not unless she's seen the foxes.

I peer at the shed, hoping Hurriyah's got enough sense to keep her cubs hidden while Mrs Mitchell and her funny scent are hanging around. When I see the mess there, my heart starts pounding. The bags are all ripped, and the rubbish is strewn around the garden. An animal's obviously got to them, either playing or looking for food, and from the big angry crease in

Mrs Mitchell's forehead, she's not going to stand for it.

"Something's going on out here Caylin, and I'm going to get to the bottom of it."

Mrs Mitchell turns her big NHS X-ray specs on me, and I can feel myself shrivelling up as she hobbles away back down the close.

I should have told her about the party. Reema's mum asked me to invite her, but I lied and said Mrs Mitchell was going to her bingo instead. The old witch feels left out and now she's looking for a way to get even. I have a bad feeling our foxes are going to pay the price for me being mean.

28
Reema

"You're not giving us enough of a start!" Zoe complains to me as we head back to the dressing room after our final afternoon's practice. "You have to get the baton to me faster!"

I am not good as the first runner in our relay races. I am faster when I am being chased or when I am chasing others. I need my brother behind me or else the fear of the big black dog to make my feet fly.

Caylin insists on running the final leg in both races. This works well for the one hundred metres, but even with me giving the team a strong start in the four hundred, by the time Caylin is handed the baton, there is too much ground to be made up for us to come close to winning.

"Reema's faster than you, Zoe!" Caylin leaps to my defence. "And anyway, what's the point when Lisa keeps dropping the baton trying to pass it to me? We're going to lose the four hundred metres relay, so we might as well accept it and just concentrate on the other races."

Lisa and Zoe are not happy about this. The relay races are their best chance to win a medal in the competition. They sit and mutter together as they get changed, avoiding looking at us. This is not good. The competition is in two days' time and we are still not working as a team.

That is not our only problem. For the last few practices Caylin has barely tried. She is running so slowly even my little sister could beat her. Something is wrong, but she will not tell me what it is. It is as though she has already decided that she will fail and has given up. I do not know what to say to help her get her confidence back. Perhaps it is too late now.

"Are you ready to go home?" I ask Caylin when I have packed away my new sports *hijab* in my bag. Caylin shakes her head.

"You go on ahead, I'll catch up." She is moving slowly, deliberately taking her time. Lisa has already left, but Zoe is still tying her shoelaces. I do not like to leave Caylin alone with her. There is still tension between them.

"Go on, OK? I'll be there in a minute," Caylin insists, a frown starting to form on her brow. We have already argued about the foxes and about running today. I do not want to end the afternoon on another argument and fall out before Caylin's birthday tomorrow.

I walk slowly down the school hall to the main doors, but I wait there, hoping Caylin is not going to do anything that will divide our team any further. Caylin's mother has a job at a hair salon now, so Caylin will not struggle to pay for food any more and does not need to steal the way she used to. I only hope she is not finding the habit too hard to break.

After two minutes I am too restless to wait any longer.

I hurry back to the changing room, ready with an excuse about forgetting my water bottle. When I peer round the door, what I see inside is every bit as bad as I feared.

Zoe is standing with her back against the lockers and Caylin is towering over her, a ten-pound note in her hand. I am just about to run in and demand that Caylin return it when I realise Caylin is not taking the money from Zoe.

She is *giving* it to her.

"It's for my birthday," Caylin is saying gruffly, "but it's yours. Take it. I still owe you five, but you'll get it later. Promise. Here."

Caylin bundles the note into Zoe's hand. Zoe looks every bit as surprised as I do.

"And I won't do it again." Caylin sounds like every word is being dragged out of her by the worst torture imaginable. "I'm…" She takes a deep breath and tries again. "I'm *sorry*, OK?"

I do not think it is just her lisp that is making this word so hard for her to say. But she says it anyway, and it sounds as though she means it. I close the door again and tiptoe back down the hall. I do not know why Caylin is giving Zoe money and apologising. I only know that for once Caylin seems to be doing the right thing, even though she is finding it difficult, and I am proud of her.

I head to the school gate to wait for Caylin there, drumming my fingers against the metal impatiently. I want to get home. I am worried about Baba. Yesterday evening he did not go to bed, but sat up with his phone all night, his face pale as he scrolled through social-media pages on the internet. When I got up to get a glass of water at dawn, Mama was sitting up with him too. They were talking in hushed voices again, their eyes

190

wet with tears, but they told me to go back to bed and not to worry.

I think they are trying to protect me from some terrible news, but I am too afraid to ask them what it is.

The growl of an engine makes me look up. The parents collecting the other children from running practice have already gone, and the street is deserted except for one car that roars down the road and stops suddenly opposite the gate.

I blink in surprise when I see it.

It is Karen's car, the lady from the Refugee Council who still comes to see us once a week to make sure we are settling in. This is not her day for a visit though.

She jumps out of the car and comes running across the road to me, waving her hand and calling my name. When I see how agitated she is, my heart squeezes tight in my chest with fear.

Something has happened. Something bad enough that Karen has to pick me up from school.

"What is it?" I cry. "Is something wrong? Is it Mama? Has Baba had a bad seizure? Oh no! It is not little Sara?"

I think of Sara running home without me after school, chasing her friends across the road without heeding the traffic. My mind is whirling so fast I cannot understand any of Karen's words as she bundles me into the car and speeds off down the street. I finally work out that Karen is saying my parents and my sister are safe, and for a moment I think the emergency must be about the foxes. It is crazy, as neither Karen nor my family know I am looking after them, but in my fright I think perhaps they have been hurt, or worse, killed.

For the past few weeks Hurriyah and her cubs have been hunting at night, leaving the garden and exploring the estate by moonlight. Hurriyah's leg is almost healed, and I am afraid that one night they will roam too far and have an accident on the busy motorway. Between us, Caylin and I provide them with more than enough food, and that is why they return to our garden at dawn. But they are wild animals, not our pets. That is why they hunt – it is their nature.

I do not believe they are safe here. I know it is time to find them a new home. But every time I ask Caylin if there is a wildlife group or organisation we can contact to help us to move them, she gets angry and refuses to talk about it.

Perhaps now it is too late. Perhaps Mrs Mitchell has called someone to exterminate them, and now they are lying dead in the garden.

"What has happened?" I ask again. "Please, say it slowly."

"It's Jamal," Karen says without taking her eyes from the road.

I suck in a great gulp of air, my whole body going numb with shock.

Is he alive? Is he dead? Tell me! I want to yell, but I cannot get the words out. My voice catches in my throat, and all I can do is choke back the sobs that threaten to suffocate me.

When we get back to our apartment I rush through the door and straight into Mama's arms, crying and burying my head in her neck. Mama is crying too, but I am so upset it takes me a long moment to see that she is smiling through her tears.

"Mama? Is it true? Is Jamal ... ?"

"He is alive, Reema! He is calling us from a camp in Turkey. He made it to safety at last, *Al-Hamdulillah!*"

I want to say praise be to God too, but my throat is so dry and tight I can barely breathe.

"Quick!" Mama says, "He is making a video call from an aid worker's phone. Come and speak with him." She leads me to the sofa where Sara is sitting on Baba's knee. Karen's laptop is open on the coffee table before them and filling the screen is a face I have seen every night in my dreams since the bombs chased us from Aleppo.

"Jamal!" I cry, throwing myself down on the floor so my face is level with his. My brother's beard has grown long and shaggy, and his hair is tickling his ears. If I were not so lost for words I would tease him about it, but all I can say is, "You are not dead?"

It sounds like a question, and it is. I am so afraid this is all just a dream I can hardly bring myself to believe that what I am seeing is real.

"No, Little Gazelle," Jamal laughs, his eyes lighting up with joy when he sees me, "I am not dead, just very tired of travelling. How are you?"

I want to say that I am well, that I am safe and settling into this new country at last. I want to tell him about Caylin, about our foxes and about the running competition. But I cannot. I am sobbing too hard to say anything more than his name over and over again. Mama puts her arms round me and holds me tight, and Baba gives my hand a gentle squeeze.

"How… how…?" I try to ask.

It is not a very clever question, but as always, my big brother understands me. "Baba tracked me down." He leans close to the screen, blocking out the view of the dusty tent he is sitting in. "I knew you would find me," he says, looking straight at Baba. "I knew you would not give up on me. It is what kept me going even when it seemed I would never make it to safety. I knew that if I could get someone to post a message on the internet you would eventually track me down. Thank you for keeping your faith, Baba. Thank you for believing in me."

Jamal's voice is thick and his eyes are wet, but the smile he gives us is bright as a rainbow when the sun comes out after a storm.

"I would never give up on you, my precious son, never."

There are tears running down Baba's cheeks too, but I have never seen him look happier. All this time I thought Baba was weak and helpless, when he was the strongest and most determined of us all. He was not hiding from the world in our apartment but spending every moment searching for his lost son. He did not give up on his faith like I feared but prayed so hard for Jamal's safety that he believed in nothing else.

Despite his wheelchair and wasted muscles, Baba is still the rock that supports us all.

"You are so far away Jamal." Sara reaches out a hand to touch the face on the computer screen. "When will you come home to us?"

"Soon, little sister, I will be home soon." Jamal lays his own hand on the screen against hers.

Home. This time I do not correct them. When Jamal is here with us, wherever we are, we will be *home.*

Mama and Baba lay their hands on Sara's too, and when I join them, my own trembling fingers touching Jamal's, I can almost hear my brother's heart beat in time with my own. We may be thousands of miles apart, but now we are all together in this room, and no time or distance or memory of war can ever divide us.

Our family is no longer broken, and I am whole again.

29
Caylin

I thought I'd never have a good birthday again when Grandad died, but I was wrong about that too. Today has been so fantastic I don't want it to end.

It started with Reema and Sara running up to my flat this morning all excited and crying that their brother was alive and they were going to see him again in a few months when they got all the paperwork sorted for him to come and live here. I ended up crying happy tears too, which is weird because he's not even my brother.

Mum made pancakes with whipped cream and chocolate for us to celebrate, and I had the best birthday breakfast ever. We were going to go to the cinema with Reema and Sara, but Brian offered to take us all out to the seaside for the day in his car. I said no at first. I didn't want to share my special day with Brian and have Johnny tagging along. But Mum talked me into it and I'm glad she did. We had a great time at the beach, and Mum giggled so much when Brian chased her into the cold water I nearly died laughing.

Maybe Brian being around and making her smile for the first time in ages isn't such a bad thing after all.

On the way home we stopped at Michael's Superchippy. We had a great party eating Syrian food with the Haddads a couple of weeks ago, and I wanted to share something from Scotland with Reema and Sara. I asked Brian to get them a black pudding or haggis supper, but he said they weren't allowed to eat meat that wasn't *halal*, from their own Muslim butchers. I was disappointed, but Brian winked at me and asked the guy serving us for a deep-fried Mars Bar each for pudding.

Now we're sitting on our sofa, eating chips and deep-fried chocolate bars, and I can't stop laughing at Reema's impression of a Glaswegian accent when she says "pure dead brilliant!" and takes a swig of Irn Bru from her can.

"Does this mean I'm Scottish now?" Sara asks, licking the chocolate off her fingers. "Am I properly Scottish?"

Brian can see that Reema doesn't like her saying that, so he says quickly, "You're Syrian-Scottish, Sara. You get to be two things at once, which is extra special as most of us only get to be from one place, and that's boring." Brian's good that way. He knows how to say the right thing and make people feel more relaxed. I was totally wrong about him. He isn't a bit like Mum's old boyfriends.

"Syrian-Scottish? Yes, I like that," Reema smiles and clinks her Irn Bru can against mine like it's champagne we're drinking. "When Jamal is here we must give him deep-fried Mars Bars so he can be Syrian-Scottish too. And we can—"

"What was that?" Mum jumps up from her chair so fast she nearly knocks over a pile of plates.

"It's probably just the TV from next door," Brian shrugs.

"Your neighbours must be half-deaf the way they need it up at full volume all the time."

But then the noise comes again, and this time we all hear it. It doesn't sound like a TV, and it isn't coming from next door. It's the sound of an animal howling in pain outside.

Reema and I exchange panicked glances, then throw down our Irn Bru cans and bolt for the door.

When we get downstairs we see something so awful it makes me feel sick.

Mrs Mitchell's standing outside the entrance to our flats, looking at a dark shape lying on the path. Darren Bradshaw's there with his big dog, but as soon as he sees Brian coming down the stairs behind us he walks away, pulling his dog with him. It has blood round its muzzle that glistens in the streetlights.

"Oh no!" Reema cries, running down the path and crouching on the grass.

I walk over slowly, my feet dragging the whole way. I know what's happened already, and I almost can't bring myself to look.

"I knew there was something funny going on in that back garden." Mrs Mitchell's face is all smug. "It's this wild animal here that's been messing up the bins and making the close stink. I scrubbed the floors twice last week and they still smell! If the Council put in doors like they promised after that vandalism weeks ago, we wouldn't have wild beasts prowling round in here at night. Just as well Darren's dog got to it really, before it took the hand off some wee kid who thought it was a puppy."

I don't hear what she's saying. I'm crouching down by the

dead fox cub too, stroking its fur and sobbing so hard I can't see anything through the blur of tears.

At first I think it's Amal, the one that Reema named. Then I realise she's too small and has darker patches round her eyes. It's Amber, the cub I named after the girl I might have been. Her red fur is all matted with blood, and I want to pick her up and hug her to my chest. Reema stretches out her hand to touch her too, even though she knows she's not supposed to.

Brian picks up the limp body before she can reach it. "I'll get rid of this," he says.

"Where are you taking her?" I want to know, but Mum's got me by the hand and is marching us all upstairs.

"It's alright Caylin, it's just a fox, not a puppy. They don't belong near people's houses. Don't worry, Brian will sort it out. Come on upstairs and finish your birthday tea, pet."

She doesn't understand, and that means I can't tell her about the rest of the foxes in case she sides with Mrs Mitchell. We were having such a good day, and now my birthday dinner tastes of nothing but guilt and sadness, heavy as a stone in the pit of my stomach.

"We shouldn't have gone out all day and left them," I mutter to Reema when Mum takes Johnny away to give him a shower and Sara goes into the kitchen to look for more juice. "It was too long for them to be on their own. They were probably hunting for food when that dog sniffed them out. If I'd just—"

"No, your mother is right," Reema interrupts, brushing away her tears. "The foxes are not safe here Caylin, you know it is true. We have talked about this. If we want them to live we must call a group who can help move them to a new home where there are no dogs and cars and—"

"What do you know about it?" I snap. "You're just trying to get rid of them because you can't be bothered with them any more! You've never cared about them as much as me! You won't even touch them!"

"That is not fair Caylin," Reema says softly.

I shut my mouth, biting my tongue so hard I taste the sharp tang of blood between my teeth. She's right, and for a moment I almost hate her for it. Then I see how sad she is too, and instead I want to give her a hug. She gives my arm a squeeze.

"We will talk about it tomorrow, after the competition, yes? We will make a plan so that no one ever hurts our foxes again."

Our foxes.

Yes.

Our foxes.

It's our job to keep them safe.

"It is late," Reema says sadly. "I must go home now. Sleep well for the competition, Caylin. Sara? Come here, it is time for us to leave."

I'd been having such a good day I'd completely forgotten about the running competition tomorrow. Now I remember, and my guts tangle up in a big knot of nerves.

Sara comes out of the kitchen with crumbs round her mouth and an orange patch of juice staining her T-shirt, and she whines and grumbles to Reema all the way down the stairs about how she wanted to finish the last piece of birthday cake. I'm wrapping it up for her in a paper towel in the kitchen when

Brian comes back in to wash his hands and pour a cup of tea. There's blood on his fingers and down the sleeve of his shirt, and it makes me sick to see it.

Amber is dead, and Hurriyah's lost another wee cub because I wasn't there to keep her safe from Darren's dog. Sometimes I'm so useless I want to scream.

I've forgotten that Brian and Johnny are staying over till I go back to my room and see Mum tucking Johnny up in a sleeping bag on the floor. She asked me this morning if it was alright, and because I was in a good mood I said yes. I wish I hadn't now. I want to cry without anyone watching.

When Mum closes the door I pull the covers up over my head so Johnny knows not to pester me to read him a story. I usually like reading to him, though I pretend I don't. He's the only kid who doesn't laugh at my lisp and he actually thinks I'm a good storyteller. Just goes to show how stupid he is.

I can still see the glow of my bedside lamp through the quilt, but that's not what's bothering me. Something feels different, wrong. Something's missing. I reach under my pillow and find a big empty space where my photo album should be.

"You wee thief! Give it back!"

I throw off the covers to find Johnny sitting on the edge of my bed leafing through my precious pictures of Gran and Grandad. He's just out of the shower and his fingers are clean for once, but that doesn't stop me wanting to thump him.

"That's mine!"

I try to snatch it off him, but he holds it out of reach, his eyes all wide like a puppy begging for table scraps. "Aw, please can

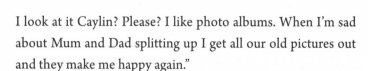

I look at it Caylin? Please? I like photo albums. When I'm sad about Mum and Dad splitting up I get all our old pictures out and they make me happy again."

I heave a big sigh like I'm still angry, but all the fight goes out of me and I let him keep hold of the album. I'd almost forgotten his life isn't perfect either. We have that in common at least, even if I'm the only one of us who knows how to tie my shoelaces and blow my own nose.

"That's you, isn't it?" Johnny points to the photo of the wee girl holding out a peanut for the squirrel. "Who's that lady with you?"

"That's my gran," I tell him, stroking the edge of the picture.

"What was she like?"

"I don't remember, but everyone says I'm just like her. I don't think so though."

"How do you know if you can't remember her?"

"I just *know*, OK?" I roll my eyes at him. "Enough with the questions already, it's time to go to sleep." I try to take the album again, but he's not ready to let it go yet.

"Hey!" he cries, all excited now as he peers at the picture. "I know where this is! See that water fountain in the corner? That's in Ravensholm Park, isn't it? I used to go there with my mum and dad for picnics. I played on the swings and fed the ducks on the pond, and one time I even saw a fox that—"

"You saw a fox in Ravensholm Park?" I say so sharply Johnny cringes like he's scared he's done something wrong.

"Yeah, and it wasn't a dead fox like the wee baby one outside. It was running through the trees fast as a rocket. I wanted to run and catch it so I could take it home and look after it, but Dad said it belonged in the wild. Have you ever seen a fox, Caylin? Before tonight I mean?"

The weight of all my worries has got so heavy it's almost crushing me – Grandad, Mum, the competition, the foxes – I can't carry it all by myself any longer. Johnny knows what it's like to have his family fall apart. He'll understand why we need to keep this family of foxes safe.

I take a deep breath. "Johnny," I say. "Can you keep a secret?"

The Fox

Death in the air, the shadows are stirring.
  The smell of my lost one hangs faint on the wind.
   Something familiar calls from the small-box.
   I pad over softly and sniff round inside.

   Piles of decay, guts-rotting, mess-spewing.
   I search through the scraps for the one I can't find.
   I know Three is in there, plastic-graved, hidden.
   I turn from the small-box and cry to the moon.

  The danger grows daily, we cannot stay longer,
  Or soon all my others will join Three and Five.
It is my job to save them, my duty to teach them.
My dream is to run with them, close by their side.

Summer is coming, sky-singing, grass-warming.
Now we must search for a place to call home.
Move to the forest, move to the river.
  Move while One, Two and Four still remain.

  The season has come.
   It is time, it is time.
  Yes, the season has come.
  It is time.

30
Reema

"Shhh, softly, do not scare them." I pull Sara's hand back so she does not touch the three small foxes that are climbing over their mother to greet us.

"Why are they living behind the shed?" Johnny asks, taking the bowl of corned beef from Caylin and putting it down on the ground for them.

"Because their mother was hurt and couldn't dig them a den," Caylin explains. "But we're going to make sure they get a new home, somewhere safe. Isn't that right Reema?"

I smile at her, but she does not look happy, only determined.

When she came knocking on our door with Johnny so early this morning I thought she had gone mad. Before I could ask her what the matter was she launched into a rushed speech – how she had been wrong about Hurriyah and knows now the foxes need to be moved somewhere safe. She even apologised for being angry with me last night, which was not like her at all.

"Go and get Sara so she can see them too," Caylin told me. "I've told Johnny about them, so now we have to call the wildlife group when we get back from the competition, don't we Reema?"

I knew then what she was doing. We had not told anyone else

about the foxes in case they gave our secret away. Caylin wanted Sara and Johnny to see them so she could not change her mind later about asking a wildlife group to help us move them. Sharing our secret was her way of letting them go and saying goodbye.

It is what I want, but it makes me sad too.

"They're so pretty," Sara says, pouring the bottle of milk into the plastic bowl when they have finished the meat. Do you *have* to get someone to take them away?"

"Yes, it isn't safe here," Caylin nods. "You're not meant to take them away from the place where they live and hunt, but we don't have a choice now. Darren's dog killed the wee one we called Amber last night, and when their mother came here to hide it looked like she'd been hit by a car or something. They're not going to survive in Drumhill. Mrs Mitchell's sniffing around, and if she sees Hurriyah she'll have Pest Control out to kill them in a shot."

"*Hurriyah!*" Sara grins. "Yes. I like that name."

"This one is called Amal." I point to the biggest cub, who is chewing Caylin's fingers looking for more meat.

"'Hope'? Yes, that is good too."

"And those are Jack and Barney," Caylin tells her. "They're named after—"

"There you are!" a voice from the corridor calls. "What are you doing out there?"

Caylin pushes the foxes back behind the shed and we all run inside before her mother comes out.

"Just doing some warm-ups for the competition," Caylin says innocently.

"At this time?" Mrs Todd does not believe it, but she is standing in her dressing gown and slippers and does not want to go outside to investigate. "Go and get ready girls," she tells me and Sara. "The taxi will be here in an hour to pick you up. Come on Caylin, time for breakfast. Your gran always said she ate a bowl of porridge before a big race to give her energy."

When her mother says this Caylin's face goes pale and she clutches her stomach as though she has a bellyache.

I do not know what porridge is, but I do not think it is the thought of this strange food that is making Caylin look so sick. Something is worrying her, something about her grandmother and the competition that has been stopping her from trying hard in our training sessions. I wish she would talk to me and let me try to help her. I am afraid the worries she is carrying will be too heavy to let her run fast today.

If she does not do well, with her family and the whole school watching, I do not think Caylin will ever want to run again.

Caylin and Johnny follow her mother upstairs, and I tiptoe back into my apartment with Sara before Mama sees we have snuck out. The next hour is a whirl of breakfast and dressing and morning *salat*, and I make sure I say an extra-special prayer for courage for the competition.

"The taxi has come!" Sara runs from the window where she has been watching the street. "Come on Baba, it is time to go and watch Reema run!"

Baba is looking good today. He has taken care to shave well and is wearing a smart shirt and trousers. His eyes are sparkling and I can see he is almost as excited as Sara. He is taking his wheelchair as it will be a long day for him, but he does not seem embarrassed to go outside in it any more. Karen has promised to meet us at the stadium. She is going to stand by the side of the track and make a video call to Jamal while I am running so he can watch my races.

The thought of my big brother being right there with me on the biggest day of my life in Scotland makes me want to sing with happiness.

"Do you have everything Reema?" Mama fusses as we push Baba down the wheelchair ramp. "Your new *hijab*, does it fit well? And your spare socks, are they packed in your bag? And—"

"'*Ihda'i*, Mama!" I laugh. "Calm down, I have everything I need." I smooth the edges of the blue sports *hijab* I am wearing, showing Mama that it fits perfectly. I will run like the wind in this.

Mrs Todd comes down the stairs with Caylin and she gets into the taxi with my parents and Sara. She is going to help them find their way in the sports stadium, as I have to go to the changing rooms with the rest of my team.

"Where is Brian?" I ask Caylin as the taxi drives off, leaving us standing alone in the street.

"Don't worry, he's coming. He just nipped to the shops with Johnny to get some juice and crisps for the competition. To be honest I think he just wanted out of the way — Mum was fussing so much over my sports kit."

Caylin tells me not to worry, but her own face is so anxious and her fists are clenched so tight with nerves I am worried she will snap. I try to think of a joke to make her feel better.

"I bet my mother fusses worse," I say, copying the way Caylin talks.

"I bet she doesn't," Caylin shoots back. "Two Mars Bars says mine is worse."

"Three. And you will lose. My mother is a champion fuss-mum."

"Four. And fuss-mum's not even a word," Caylin laughs.

For a moment her face relaxes, the tension draining away. But when we go to sit on the low wall by the path to wait for Brian to pick us up, Caylin's hand clutches at her stomach again as though she is trying to hold herself together.

While we are checking our sports bags one last time to make sure we have everything we need, Mrs Mitchell comes out and stands looking down the street with us.

"Morning girls, going running are you?"

I can see Caylin's face creasing back into a big scowl, so I smile politely. "Yes Mrs Mitchell, today is our running competition."

"That's good," she nods, "I was hoping you two wouldn't be around while it happened. I wouldn't want you to be upset, but it has to be done, you know."

I am not sure I understand her words, but Caylin's eyes go wide with fright and she jumps off the wall, yelling, "What have you done?"

"We can't have wild animals running around the garden, biting people and giving us all diseases!" Mrs Mitchell frowns. "So don't be silly about it Caylin. After I found that mangy thing out here last night I went looking for the mother. Is that what you two have been up to back there? It's disgusting, no wonder the bins are always in such a state."

Caylin looks like she is ready to launch herself at Mrs Mitchell, but just then I grab her arm and point to the van that is turning into our street. My English is not fluent yet, but I can read some of the words that are painted on the side of the van and guess what they mean.

Pestifix
Pest Control
Safe and clean extermination services

Caylin gives a cry of horror and goes running back down the path. I am only a heartbeat behind her.

"Don't be silly girls!" Mrs Mitchell calls after us. "They need to be got rid of!"

"What do we do?" Caylin asks when we reach the shed. "Reema, what are we going to do?" Her voice is shaking and she picks up Amal, who has come running out to meet her, hugging the cub to her chest.

Now is not the time for me to be angry at her for training the cubs to trust people like pet dogs. Now is the time to *think*. My eyes dart round the garden, at the piles of rubbish the foxes have been treating as their playground. There must be something here that can help us save them.

My eyes come to rest on the boxes strewn round the garden, and I know what we must do.

"Come on Reema!" Caylin urges. "What's the plan?"

"The plan is: we give them what they want."

210

A van door slams in the distance. The exterminators are coming.

"*What*?" Caylin gasps. "Are you saying I should just hand the foxes over to them?"

I have made my mind up. There is no other way. "Yes Caylin," I nod. "That is exactly what you must do."

31
Caylin

"There! In the box! Those are the beasts I called you about!"

Mrs Mitchell points to the big box I'm carrying as I come running down the path.

Before I can escape across the road a tall man in overalls steps in front of me and grabs hold of it.

"Not so fast pet. I need to take them. It's kinder in the long run."

"What are you going to do with them?" I ask nervously, refusing to let go.

"Don't worry, they won't feel a thing. They're not going to suffer. Oof, this is heavy – how many are there, four? I'm just going to put this in the back of the van, OK?"

Another man wearing green Pestifix overalls gets out of the van and starts walking towards me. There's nowhere to run. I'm out of options.

"Can I put it in myself? Please? I want to say goodbye."

The men exchange glances, but they don't want a fuss, so they nod and lead me across the road, careful not to take their eyes off me for a single moment in case I try to escape with my box of foxes.

Mrs Mitchell is peering after me, and I swear there's a smug look of satisfaction in her mean wee eyes.

Evil witch, I think, dragging my feet all the way across the road.

The men open the van and help me set the box down inside. There's cages and bottles of poison and gas masks and sharp-looking tools back there. It looks like an animal torture chamber. One of the men sees my eyes go wide and says, "Don't fuss pet, we'll take good care of them."

I know exactly how he's going to 'take care' of my foxes and I want to punch him for being so cruel.

"Should we move them to the cages?" the younger guy asks the man, who looks like his boss.

"Nah, they might escape. Just ride in the back with them John, and keep that box lid shut."

I take a step back, thinking they're done with me. But just as the younger guy jumps in the back and his boss goes to close the door, they take a quick look inside the box to count the foxes. That's when all hell breaks loose.

"Hey! It's just full of stones!"

Time to go! I decide.

Before they can grab me by the T-shirt I take off down the road, my legs pumping so hard I'd qualify for the Olympics if I was old enough. The men don't know whether to follow me or go looking for the foxes in the back yard, and by the time they've decided I'm already halfway to the dual carriageway and well out of sight. I don't slow down till I reach the bus stop by the chip shop. I collapse on the bench, my legs shaking and my lungs burning.

"Are they coming?" Reema asks.

She's sitting there waiting for me, a big box just like mine on the ground in front of her. She's struggling to keep the lid closed; the foxes don't like being all squashed up and shoogled around inside, but I bet they'd like the cages in the back of the exterminators' van even less.

"I think we're all clear," I pant. "How'd you get here so fast?"

"You forget Caylin, I am the White Gazelle." Reema smiles at me, but there's so much worry in her face it looks like a frown. "Where do we go now?"

She was the one who came up with the idea of climbing over the wall and escaping with the real box of foxes that I passed over to her. While I was busy distracting the exterminators she was running off down the back alley with Hurriyah and her cubs. Now it's my turn to come up with something clever to save them.

"Johnny was looking at my old photos last night," I think aloud. "There's one of my gran and me when I was just a wee girl, and—"

"Pictures will not help the foxes!" Reema snaps. "We need a plan!"

"I know!" I yell back. "But there's one of me and Gran feeding squirrels in Ravensholm Park, not too far from here. Grandad and Mum wouldn't take me back there after she died because it made them too sad, but Johnny used to go there with his mum and dad as well, and he said he saw a fox there once. I don't remember much about it, but I know there's lots of trees and green spaces and a duck pond, and there's even a wee river running through the woods. It's the perfect place for Hurriyah and her cubs to live."

"Alright," Reema nods, even though I'm not sure she's understood everything I just said. "How do we get there?"

"That's how." I point to the bus that's coming down the dual carriageway towards us. It's been so long since I rode the bus to Ravensholm Park with Gran and Grandad I'm not sure I can remember the way, but there's no time now to worry about getting lost.

Besides, I'm not alone. I've got Reema and the foxes with me, and we'll make it to safety together, no matter what.

32
Reema

We have been on the bus for only ten minutes and already our plan is going badly wrong. The foxes are restless, growling and fighting to get out of their box. We have tucked it into the wheelchair space, but even with both our feet resting on top to keep the lid down, the strong scent of fox is beginning to fill the crowded bus. The other passengers are starting to mutter about us more and more loudly, and I can see the bus driver watching us in his mirror with a frown on his face. We had to leave our sports bags behind when we rescued the foxes, and Caylin only had enough money in her pocket to pay for us to ride a few stops. The driver is starting to wonder when we are going to get off, and we are getting more nervous with each passing moment.

"Maybe we can stop and find a phone," I whisper again. "We can call—"

"Who?" Caylin whispers anxiously back. "Brian? I don't have his number! Mum's broken the new phone Brian bought her already, and I bet you don't know your dad's number, so who exactly are we meant to call, huh?"

I can feel tears stinging my eyes, and I look away. It was not supposed to be like this.

We were going to have such a wonderful time today. Caylin and I would have won medals in the competition and our families would be so proud of us. We would have celebrated together, then we would have called a wildlife group and arranged for them to help resettle Hurriyah and her cubs. We would have gone with them to their new home and set them free, but the wildlife group would have tracked them so we would have been able to visit them and bring them treats.

It was all going to be perfect.

Now it is such a disaster my head hurts to think of it.

We are already late for the competition and our families will be wondering where we are. Brian will be frantically searching for us, and Miss Lindsey and our teammates will be furious with us for letting them down. Even if we get to this place called Ravensholm Park and release Hurriyah and her cubs, we will lose them forever. Then we will be stranded, as we do not have the bus fare to get ourselves home.

"We will miss our races," I say sadly. "We will disappoint our families and our team and our whole school."

And I am going to let Jamal down, I think. That is what hurts the most. I wish he was here right now holding my hand. He would know exactly what to do. He would come up with a plan that would save the foxes and get us back to the sports stadium in time to run our races. Caylin only has half a plan, and right now she's refusing to work as a team.

"It doesn't matter about the stupid sports competition!"

Caylin hisses. "All that matters is getting our foxes to safety. Who cares if we don't run some pointless races? The other schools are way better than us, we'd just lose anyway."

I see the way her shoulders hunch and her hand rubs her stomach as though the butterflies in there have claws and are trying to tear their way out. I see the guilt in her eyes and the way she sighs in relief at the thought of missing her races, and I realise she would rather be anywhere else than the sports stadium right now.

"Caylin Todd!" I growl, just like Hurriyah, "you have already given up! You must not—"

"Sshh!" Caylin grabs my arm suddenly, silencing me. Something is happening. The bus is slowing down.

"Are we arrived?" I whisper, looking out of the window doubtfully. We are coming to a busy intersection. Here there are only traffic lights and lorries and concrete and not a blade of grass in sight. This is not Ravensholm Park. "Caylin, where are we?"

Caylin adjusts her feet on the box of struggling foxes and looks out of the window too. "I think this is Lairdsland Cross," she frowns. "I think the park is around here somewhere."

"Are you sure?"

"No. I haven't been here since I was about five."

Caylin looks like she wants to cry, but she bites her lip and tries to be brave when the bus stops at a shelter near the traffic lights. Then the driver opens his door and calls down the aisle, "OK you two, enough wasting my time. You've had a free ride for the last couple of miles, it's time you got out."

There is nothing we can do. We shuffle along the aisle with

our box and down the steps, trying to keep the lid on as tight as we can. Before Caylin can beg the driver to let us stay on the bus a little longer, he closes the door behind us and drives away. We are left standing alone beside a noisy junction that looks a million miles away from the peaceful park Caylin described.

"Now what do we do?" I ask. I have run out of ideas.

Caylin helps me set the box down, and even though she does not know who to call, she goes to try the phone that is hanging in an old phone box by the shelter. After pressing a few buttons and listening hard, she drops the handset in disgust. "It's well dead," she mutters. "Probably hasn't worked in years. No one needs phones like this any more, they've all got mobiles."

"I do not have a mobile phone," I say.

"Yeah, thanks for pointing that out Reema, that's really helpful."

Caylin can be nasty when she is in a bad mood, and her scowl is so deep it looks as though a thunderstorm is brewing behind her eyes. She does not like feeling helpless. It makes me feel sad, but it makes her feel angry, and Caylin Todd is dangerous when she is angry.

"Perhaps—" I begin, but before I can speak another word the lid of the box flies open and one of the fox cubs comes leaping out before I can grab her.

"Stop the rest!" Caylin yells, throwing herself at the cub and trying to catch her. I sit on the box to make sure Hurriyah and the other two cubs cannot escape, but it is Amal who is free and she is fast and sneaky. She dodges Caylin's hands and goes running out into the middle of the road, right into the oncoming traffic.

"Amal!" Caylin cries, running blindly across the road after her. There is a car coming so fast it is just a blur. I hear a screech of tyres and a loud scream, then my whole field of vision is filled with red, the colour of blood.

33
Caylin

The red car stops just inches from my face.

I'm lying on the ground, holding on to Amal so tightly I can feel her heart pounding just as fast as my own.

A car door opens and someone comes running out. I feel big hands under my arms and then I'm lifted to my feet.

"Are you OK pet?" a familiar voice asks. I look up. It's Brian, and it's his red car that almost knocked me over. I'm so glad I want to hug him, but I'm afraid to let go of Amal for even a second.

"Get onto the pavement, quickly!" Brian carries me to safety as the other cars slow down and honk their horns behind us. I stumble back to the bus shelter, where Reema is still sitting on the box. Her face is so pale she looks likes she's going to faint. I wrestle Amal back into the box, then I sit down on it with Reema before my legs collapse.

Brian's car pulls into the bus lane and parks there, and Johnny comes jumping out before Brian can stop him.

"I knew you'd be here!" he cries, throwing his arms round me and giving me a sticky hug. "Mrs Mitchell said you'd run off with the foxes and I knew you'd take them to Ravensholm Park after I saw your pictures last night Caylin, I just *knew* it!"

I hug him, and I don't even mind for once that he's all smug and proud of himself and his snotty nose is pressed into my cheek.

"What did you think you were doing?" Brian shakes his head at us. "Reema, your parents will be half-daft with worry! Come on, let's get you to the stadium. Use my phone to call your dad, Reema, and tell him we're on our way now to—"

"No!"

Reema says it so suddenly it makes me jump.

"We are not going back yet. We must find the foxes a new home. Somewhere they are safe. Somewhere they can be free."

Reema's on my side and fighting so hard for our foxes I could hug her. I know how badly she wants to run in the competition, but she cares about our foxes more than anything.

"Please Brian?" I plead. "Mrs Mitchell called the exterminators, and if we take them back they'll be killed. Can you give us a lift to Ravensholm Park first so we can let them go there?"

"But what about your races, pet?" Brian frowns. "You've been practising so hard for them, and your mum'll be so disappointed if—"

"I don't care! I just want the foxes to be safe! *Please?*"

"OK then girls, get in the car – the park's just up the road," Brian sighs, and I jump up and give him a big hug too. He helps us move the box onto the back seat, where Reema and I can keep the lid securely closed between us, and he drives to the junction, turning left at the traffic lights.

"It is lucky we do not go any further on the bus," Reema says, "It is going the wrong way."

I'm too distracted to answer her. I've got my face pressed up against the window as we drive through another set of traffic lights, then take the dual carriageway round a big bend that passes under a bridge. Everything's starting to look strangely familiar, like a dream I had a long time ago. There's a line of tall trees along the road to the right, and suddenly I sit up straight, a shiver running through my spine like I've just had an electric shock.

"There!" I yell. "That road there! Turn right Brian, that's the road to the park!"

"I know pet, I've been here before too." Brian grins at me in the mirror and turns up a quiet road that leads to a big set of iron gates. As soon as I see them, I know we've come to the right place. The park doesn't just look familiar, it feels familiar too.

When the car stops I jump out and hurry on ahead, leaving Brian to carry the box full of growling foxes. My fingers start tingling as I reach the heavy gates and look up the hill that winds through the woodland.

It's still there. The water fountain halfway up the hill. The one I used to race to when I came here with Gran. Maybe I haven't lost all my memories of her after all. Maybe they've just been left behind here in Ravensholm and I can find them if I look hard enough.

My heart beats so hard with hope I feel dizzy.

"Race you to the fountain," I challenge Reema when she

catches up. "Last one there's a rotten egg." Those aren't my words. They belong to my gran.

"What?" Reema blinks, but I've already taken off, running up the hill like my life depends on it. The wind's whispering in the trees and it sounds like my gran's voice calling to me: "*Caylin! Caylin!*" I can almost hear her laughter behind me as I go stumping up the hill on my short legs, kicking up the leaves with my bright red welly boots.

My legs are much longer now though and I get to the wee metal fountain in six seconds flat. I grab the handle, eager to see the water gushing up and sparkling in the sunlight like it does in my memory, but the fountain's all rusty and the handle won't turn. It's old and useless now.

"Caylin! What are you doing?" Reema comes running up to join me, looking all worried like she thinks I've gone mad.

"Nothing. Just… nothing."

I force myself to forget about chasing the ghosts in my head and focus on why we're here. Our foxes need to be set free, and that's going to hurt even worse than finding my memories are as out of date as the corned beef I used to nick from the Drumhill Spar.

Brian catches up with the box and we walk on till we come to the dense woodland that runs round one side of the pond. It's dark and quiet in there, with plenty of places for a fox family to hide.

"This is where we used to come for picnics with Mum when I was wee, isn't it?" Johnny asks his dad. Brian nods, but his smile's a bit sad.

"I think it is time to say goodbye," Reema says. "This is the right place. It is so beautiful and peaceful here."

"Yeah, it's not bad," I agree. "You think they'll be happy here? Hurriyah and her cubs?"

"I think this is perfect," Reema smiles. I want to smile back and be brave just like her, but I can feel my bottom lip trembling. Brian notices and puts his arm round me.

"It's not a big park Caylin. If we come here for a day out with your mum then you might see your foxes again."

I give his arm a squeeze. It's the closest I can get to saying thank you for being so nice to me.

"What about the wildlife group?" Reema asks as Brian puts the box down on the grass. "Maybe we can call them anyway? Perhaps they can watch over Hurriyah and her cubs to make sure they have enough food here."

"Good idea," Brian nods. "I'll give them a call later and let them know where we've released them."

"Can I help?" Johnny comes bounding over as we open the box, but Brian lifts him onto his shoulders where he can watch without disturbing us.

"Let the girls do it," he says softly. "They need to say goodbye."

I want to cuddle each of the fox cubs before we let them go, but I don't get the chance. As soon as Reema and I lift the lid they all tumble out, growling and snapping and running for the trees. Hurriyah makes sure all of her cubs have escaped before she chases after them. Her leg is looking a lot better and she's not limping the way she used to.

"Wait!" I call. "Come back! I haven't said goodbye."

I follow them, but I can't see anything through the thick bushes. Reema catches my arm before I can go plunging into the dense woodland in search of them.

"Let them go," she whispers. "It is time."

I nearly snap something nasty at her, but when I turn round there's a big tear running down her face and her lip is trembling too.

I grab her hand and hold it tight, and we're just about to leave when I feel something wet touch my other hand. I look down, and just for a moment I see Hurriyah's head poking out of a bush. She gives my hand another quick lick, and then she's gone, disappearing back into the woods with her cubs.

This time I know she's gone for good.

"They'll get lost in there," I sniff. "We'll never see them again."

"No," Reema smiles sadly, "they are not lost Caylin. They are free."

We're just turning to go when the sparkle of sunlight on water catches my eye. A swan is flapping its wings on the pond as it gets ready to fly. The surface of the water shatters into a thousand pieces, like a broken mirror reflecting the bright blue sky.

And suddenly I remember.

"Wait for me Gran!"

I'm running by the water, but my legs are too short and I'm falling far behind. The woman in the yellow dress is too fast. I feel small and alone and I want to cry with frustration.

"Gran! Don't go! *Please?*"

The woman turns, and this time I see her face clearly. She has bright red hair just like Mum, and her smile is so wide it wraps me up in its warmth.

"Come on Caylin! Catch up! You can do it!"

She's holding her hand out to me and I try as hard as I can to reach it, desperate to prove I'm as fast as her. When her fingers close over mine I can feel the spark that travels between us, connecting us across time.

"Come on pet. Let's chase the wind."

Gran takes off again, and this time I run by her side, keeping pace with her until the trees are flashing past and the sky is just a shimmer of blue on the water. Gran hasn't gone on ahead and left me behind. She's right here with me, lending me her speed as she holds my hand so tight I know I'll never be alone again.

"Caylin?"

"*Caylin?*"

"CAYLIN?"

Reema has to say it three times before I finally hear her.

"What?" I blink, shaking my head slowly like I'm waking from a dream. When I look down I realise it's not Gran's hand I'm holding, it's Reema's.

"Are you coming to the competition?"

Reema isn't just asking me if I'll go with her to the stadium. She's asking me if I'll do my best for my team and not let her down when she needs me most. For the first time in what seems like forever, the thought of racing doesn't make me feel sick or scared or weighed down with worry.

It makes me feel free.

"I'm ready," I nod, my heart beating fast with excitement. "It's time for us to run."

34
Reema

"Where have you been?" Miss Lindsey is so angry with us that her face is turning red.

"We couldn't help it!" Caylin tries to explain. "We had to save our foxes from the exterminators and take them to Ravensholm Park and—"

"Never mind that now!" Miss Lindsey holds up a hand to silence her. "If you're quick you'll just make the last race. Get changed, fast as you can. Where's your sports kit?"

Caylin and I exchange guilty glances. Our bags are still sitting on the ground outside our apartment building where we left them.

"Oh for goodness sake!" Miss Lindsey tuts. "There are some spare sports clothes in that box there, the trainers you're wearing will have to do. Hurry up though, you've only got five minutes."

She goes over to talk to Zoe and Lisa, who are sitting on the bench crying, and Caylin and I run to the other end of the locker room where a jumble of T-shirts and tracksuits are piled in a box. Zoe's tears are disappointed ones – she just missed winning a medal in her two hundred metres race. Lisa's tears are angry. Her best chance of a medal was in the one hundred metres relay race that we missed. We have spoiled this day for both of them.

Caylin and I are not in any better shape for running than our teammates are. Caylin's eyes are red from crying all the way here in the car, and I have to keep blowing my nose and swallowing hard to ease the huge lump in my throat. It would have been better if we had just gone straight home. We have no chance of a medal in the four hundred metres relay. Our team does not work together well enough for that, and now we have broken it beyond repair.

"I knew you'd let us down," Zoe mutters as we tramp down the long corridor that leads to the sports track. "You can't be trusted with anything." She is speaking to Caylin, but I know her sharp words are aimed at me too.

Before Caylin can say something angry back, I tell Zoe and Lisa about our foxes and how they would have been killed if we had not run away with them.

The girls' eyes go wide, their resentment slowly fading as they hear about the dead cubs and the Pest Control van.

"You mean you had a fox family in your back yard all this time and you didn't say anything about it?" Lisa asks Caylin. "Why didn't you tell us? We could've come and seen them and helped you feed them." She looks disappointed, and Caylin looks surprised.

"Didn't think you'd be interested," Caylin shrugs. I am not sure if she means she believes that Zoe and Lisa would be uninterested in the foxes or in spending time after school with her.

"But baby *foxes* though!" Zoe says eagerly. "How could you think we wouldn't want to see them?"

Caylin shrugs again, and this time I know what she means. She did not want to share her foxes with anyone else. Not even me.

"Look, we get why you two missed the races, and we're still mad at you," Lisa says, "but if you have any more foxes moving into your back garden, will you let us come and see them next time? Will you?" She does not look mad now. She looks eager and the tears in her eyes have dried up.

Caylin does not shrug this time. She smiles back and nods. "OK."

I am about to tell them the names of all of our foxes, but it is already time to walk down the short tunnel and out onto the sports ground. The noise of the crowd and the loudspeakers, and the coaches giving instructions to the teams that are already standing in a big group on the track waiting for us, is almost overwhelming.

For a moment I am back in Aleppo, watching a crowd of shouting protestors march against a line of soldiers. The soldiers were just supposed to keep the peace, to make sure no one got hurt on the march. But I remember the way they raised their weapons on the men and woman and students in the chanting crowd. There was a crackle of gunfire, and the smell of burning, and screams filled the air, and—

"It's OK Reema." Caylin has read the fear in my face. She is looking overwhelmed too, but her eyes are determined and she squeezes my hand. "Your mum and dad and little sister are up there in the crowd watching. There's nothing to be scared of. My gran's going to run with me today, and Jamal will be right there with you too. We're going to make them proud of us."

I take a deep breath and let all of the tension in my body go when I breathe out. Jamal will be watching me race from Karen's phone. As long as my big brother is here, then nothing will stop me from running like the wind.

"Take your places, girls," Miss Lindsey tells the big group of students as she hands out the batons. "It's time to race."

I take a baton, but before I can go to the starting line with the others who are running the first leg, Caylin stops me.

"Wait!" she tells Zoe and Lisa. "We can't run like this."

"*What?*" Lisa cries. "Caylin Todd, if you walk away now and mess this up for us I'll—"

"Just listen!" There is a new note of authority in Caylin's voice. It is not the mumbling of a girl afraid that others will laugh at her lisp or the nasty growl of a bully who wants her own way without caring if she hurts others. No, it is the voice of someone who believes in herself for the very first time.

"We're not going to get a medal unless we change how we run this race."

"No way!" Zoe crosses her arms.

"It's too late to change now!" Lisa agrees.

But I know it is not too late to change things for the better. Caylin is standing by her team, and she will not let us down. I believe this wild fox girl can be trusted at last.

I hand the baton to Caylin and ask, "What should we do?"

35
Caylin

When the whistle blows, my whole body tenses like my muscles are going to snap. It's Zoe who moves though. She takes off like a rocket from the starting line, getting straight to the front before the other girls can react. I always said Reema should run the first bit, but that was only because I didn't want to admit that Zoe Weir was actually good at anything. She's not our best runner over a distance, not by a long way, but when it comes to getting off to a flying start she's unbeatable.

Come on, keep going!

I urge her on, seeing the other girls start to catch up as Zoe passes the two hundred metres mark. She's fast, but she doesn't have Reema's stamina. None of us do. That's why I had to change our running order at the last minute.

Just hold on!

Five of the other runners have passed Zoe by the time she gets round the bend and reaches Lisa, who's waiting for the baton. This isn't the exchange that worries me. Lisa and Zoe are best friends. They've never dropped the baton once.

Yes! That's it!

233

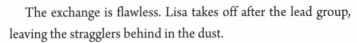

The exchange is flawless. Lisa takes off after the lead group, leaving the stragglers behind in the dust.

The chase is on.

Lisa's not like her big sister who hangs round the shops with her friends and smokes all day. Lisa wouldn't give up the chase if she flicked a cigarette at me and I ran away. She would just keep running and running until she caught me. She wouldn't slap me about the way the high-school kids sometimes do either, the way I learned to do to the younger kids. She'd just laugh at me and my lisp and my scabby clothes and make me feel like a loser.

Maybe that's why I've been so scared of her.

It's her determination to keep going and get what she wants that's keeping us in the race though. She clings to the heels of the lead runners, never letting them out of her sight for a second. She isn't going to overtake them, but she's giving us a chance, and that's the very best thing we can hope for.

She nears the corner and my heart starts pounding like a drum in my chest.

They all think I insisted on running the last leg up till now because I think I'm better than them.

I don't.

It's because I wanted someone else to blame for not running fast enough when I lost.

I know I'm the weakest link in this relay chain. I'm the best in a short race, but my baton exchange is sloppy and I don't have the heart to keep going when I'm passed by other runners. If I get handed the baton last then it's not my fault if I can't catch up.

But that's not how I want to run today, with everyone

watching. Today I don't want to prove I'm fast. Everyone knows that.

Today I want to prove I'm not a quitter.

Lisa chases the others round the second bend. Her head's up and her eyes are looking straight at me. There's no spite in them now. Today she doesn't want me to fail. Today she wants me to get it right.

I lock eyes with her and hold out my hand, ready to catch the baton she raises.

Don't drop it!

I catch the smooth piece of wood and run, hoping my grip is tight and it stays in my hand. It does. It wasn't a perfect exchange, but it was good enough.

Now all I have to do is keep going and not give up. I'm never going to win this third leg of the race. There are five girls ahead of me and there's no way I can pass them. I've never given my best in a race like this before, I've always just stopped trying. I've never seen the point when the only person I'm racing against is myself.

Maybe that's because I've never had a team cheering me on before.

I can hear Lisa behind me yelling my name and telling me, "Go! Go!"

The crowd is cheering, and although I can't hear them up there, I know Mum and Brian and Johnny and Reema's family are shouting my name too.

It makes me feel like the most important person in the whole world.

All the hurt from losing our foxes melts away, and I know that somewhere in the wild Hurriyah is running too, but not because she's afraid. We don't have to be scared of Mrs Mitchell and the exterminators any more, of roads and traffic and Darren and his dog.

All those times I felt weak and useless because I couldn't stop Mum from getting depressed and drinking don't matter now. She's proud of me for being brave and taking part today, and whether I win or lose, she's going to love me just the same. I've been so afraid of letting Mum down by not being as fast as Gran that I buried all my memories so deep I almost lost them. But when I let the foxes go at Ravensholm, I found them again.

Gran's not long gone and forgotten, she's right here, running by my side. I can hear her call to me as the wind whispers in my hair, her voice as bright as sunshine on water.

"Come on Caylin! Catch up! You can do it!"

Somewhere up there I know that Grandad's smiling too, watching me and Gran run the race of our lives together. For the first time since I can remember, I'm not running away.

This time it's my best friend I'm running to, and I can see her up ahead, standing waiting for me, her hand stretched out for mine.

36
Reema

I want to keep my mind on the race, but as I watch my teammates pass the baton, all I can think about is Jamal.

I cannot see Karen in the crowd, but I know she will be there, close to the track, holding her phone so that Jamal can watch me run. Even though it will take a few months to complete the paperwork for him to come to Scotland, he is here with me today. Whether I come in first or last, he will be equally proud of me. Knowing my big brother is just a heartbeat away has given me so much hope I am ready to burst with happiness.

Perhaps not everything I had to leave behind will be lost forever.

Now I have faith that when my country is free from war I will see it again. Brian is right: I have not lost my old culture and language here, I have just gained a new one.

Maybe one day I will see Hurriyah and her cubs again too.

But there is no more time to be sad at parting with them now. Caylin is running towards me, her face more determined than I have ever seen before. She has not dropped far behind the group like she usually does when there are others ahead of her. She has dug her heels in and kept on chasing them, catching them on the last bend and holding on to the back of the group.

She has not given up. She has kept us in the fight.

For a moment our hands touch as I take the baton, and I can almost feel the energy run down her arm and pass into mine.

"Run Reema!" she yells, dropping back and letting me take over.

It is my race now, and I must catch the runners out in front.

I grit my teeth, my legs tearing up the distance to the leading group, every nerve in my body singing. The wind does not stream through my sea-green headscarf like I am used to, there are no loose ends billowing against the blue sky. There is only the close fit of my sports *hijab*, reminding me that I am in a real race, not playing catch-me-if-you-can with my brother on the way to the *souks*.

It was Jamal who first raced with me through the streets of Aleppo, but it was Caylin who taught me that speed is not everything. Without the courage to keep going, even our fast legs will let us down. I have not forgotten what I learned.

I will win this race for all of us.

My lungs are burning, but I suck the air down despite the pain. My legs cry out, my calves ache, but I ignore it all. My vision narrows until I cannot even see the runners on either side of me any more. All that is left is the finish line and the sound of my name ringing in my ears.

"Run Reema!" Caylin does not stop yelling at me all the way down the final straight.

"Run *habibti!*" I'm sure I can hear a distant voice from the crowd.

"Run Little Gazelle!"

It is Jamal's voice I hear in my head as I cross the finish line. He has run by my side the whole way. But as I slow down and stop at the side of the track I realise the voice is not just in my head. Karen is there waiting, holding out her phone so I can see my brother's face smiling back at me.

"Yes!" Jamal is jumping up and down and punching the air. There are many people with him and they are all slapping him on the back and cheering. It looks as though the whole camp has crowded round the small screen to watch my race. "I knew you could do it Reema, I *knew* it!"

"I was running for you Jamal," I pant, "I was running for all of us." I reach out and touch hands with him again across the distance, so happy we are together on this special day I almost do not hear the official race result being called over the speakers.

I do not need to listen to it to know that I have come in first. It is obvious from the joy of my brother and the cheers of his friends in the refugee camp. It is written in the grimaces of the girls I have beaten and in the yells of excitement from my teammates who come sprinting across the grass to celebrate with me. Zoe and Lisa are crying again, but this time it is with happiness.

"You did it!" Caylin yells, throwing her arms round me. "You won!"

"No Caylin," I grin, hugging her back so tight it hurts. "*We* won."

I know now that whatever happens in my life here, I will be ready to face it.

She is the Fox Girl, and I am the White Gazelle, and together we can outrun anything.

The Fox

The wild is calling, we cry out our answer,
Barking our joy to the cloudless blue sky.
This is our refuge, this our safe haven,
  This our new territory. Here we will stay.

  The forest protects us, the water before us,
  The radiant sun climbing high overhead.
  Green grass beneath us, new life around us.
  Sunfire on water, the world is aflame.

  One, Two and Four are ready and eager,
  Tumbling, playing and fresh for the chase.
My leg is untested, still sore. Will it hold me?
But I must be brave or risk falling behind.

Now is my moment. Now I must lead them.
Now I must train them to run with the wind.
I take a deep breath of the warm summer fragrance,
  My heart fills with hope as I race for the trees.

The little ones follow me, bright-eyed, excited.
Our worries are over, we fly through the grass.
  Summoned by nature, at one with the wildness.
   This is our birthright. Now we are free.

   This could be home,
   So we run, we run.
   Yes, this could be home.
   We *run*...

Acknowledgements

My writing journey has been a real adventure, and I'd like to thank all of my family and friends who have given me help and encouragement along the way. Reema's father was her family's rock, but my rocks have been my mother and my brother Martin, whose unwavering support gave me the willpower to keep going when success seemed too far out of reach.

Huge thanks to my fabulous agent Ben Illis, who really is the best in the business. He goes above and beyond the call of duty for every one of his authors, and I couldn't have got here without him. I'd also like to thank my editors Sally Polson and Jennie Skinner for the great work they've done in helping to bring this novel to life. Their advice and suggestions have made an invaluable contribution to shaping Reema and Caylin's search for belonging.

Thanks to Nadjia Sari and Nader Alhalabi for their help in translating the Arabic phrases, and to Abdelkader Boutaleb for reading to ensure Islam was treated sensitively in this story.

Finally, thanks to the Scottish Refugee Council for collaborating on the book launch and being so generous with their time when I needed information. Their work with families like Reema's provides a much needed lifeline to those fleeing conflict and persecution, and in order to help support those who come to Scotland in search of a safer home:

20% of the author royalties for this novel will be donated to the Scottish Refugee Council.

An interview with Victoria Williamson

Where did you get the idea for this book? Why did you choose to include a refugee family?

A book is an adventure, and my first real-life adventures began when I became a teacher. I taught for a number of years in Cameroon, Malawi and China as well as the UK, and during that time I met many children whose unique stories inspired my writing.

The characters in *The Fox Girl and the White Gazelle* are composed of many voices. Caylin, a troubled twelve-year-old struggling with her mother's alcohol addiction in a Glasgow council estate, and Reema, a Syrian Muslim refugee whose world has been turned upside down by war, were inspired by some of the children I have taught.

My experiences of working with children from many different backgrounds, particularly those whose families were seeking asylum, made me realise how important it was for me to write inclusive stories where all children can see a reflection of themselves in heroic roles. When the Syrian war began, the sheer scale of the humanitarian crisis that followed was overwhelming, and like many other people I felt powerless to do anything about it. It was then that I decided to write a story about a girl whose family has fled the fighting and are trying to build a new life, and little by little Reema's character began to take shape.

Can you tell us a bit about the Scottish Refugee Council?

I found out about the Scottish Refugee Council's work when I was researching the experiences of Syrian refugees settled in Scotland. The Scottish Refugee Council works with new refugees and family members of refugees reunited in Scotland to assist them in integrating into the country. They campaign to improve the legal rights of refugees, and work very hard to help people understand the positive role that refugees can play in their new communities.

I was really impressed by the dedication of their team and the wide range of services they offer. Reading the stories of newly arrived refugees, meeting some of the fundraising team to hear more about their work, and talking in person to young refugees settled in Aberdeen, inspired me to pledge to donate twenty percent of my author royalties from *The Fox Girl and the White Gazelle* to the Scottish Refugee Council to support the important work they do.

What do you think are the main similarities and differences between Caylin and Reema?

Caylin has lost her grandparents, and with her mother's depression turning to alcoholism, she resorts to bullying other children for money and stealing to keep food on the table. She longs for the past when her grandparents were alive and she was part of a loving family. She keeps the memory of her grandmother, a talented athlete, alive through running, and rediscovers some of her happy memories of her grandfather by sharing them with Reema.

Reema has lost everything in the Syrian war, including her older brother Jamal, and she's struggling to fit in and feel safe so far from home. She runs to remember too: her memories of running through the streets of Aleppo after school with Jamal are bound up in the headscarf he bought her, and she clings on tightly to this as a symbol of everything she has lost and hopes to recover.

Despite their different cultural backgrounds, both girls have suffered loss and are searching for a sense of belonging, and it is Hurriyah, the fox called 'Freedom' who is the metaphor for the girls' struggles. Her sense of loss over her dead mate, destroyed den and injured leg which prevents her from running, hunting and caring for her vulnerable cubs mirrors the girls' struggles to overcome their own sad experiences. Her refrain, 'This is not home. It hurts,' changes into something far more hopeful at the end of the book when both Caylin and Reema realise that home isn't a place, it's the people you love.

Do you think you're more like Caylin or Reema? Did you find it easier to write in the voice of a particular character?

They're both very good at running and I'm a bit of a tortoise, so I don't think I'm like either of them in that respect!

Caylin was the first character I created for this novel, and she was in many ways the easiest, as her happy memories of Glasgow came straight from my own childhood: weekend trips to stay with my grandparents in Drumchapel, visits to feed the squirrels in nearby Dawsholm Park, and primary school sports days cheering on my gazelle-limbed best friend as she outran all the boys in our class.

Reema was a little trickier as her cultural background was very different from my own. However I realised if it was only written from Caylin's point of view, then Reema would always be seen as a Syrian Muslim 'other' through Caylin's eyes.

Without a voice of her own Reema would at best be a sidekick tagging along on Caylin's journey of self-discovery. In order to create a three-dimensional refugee character who reflected the experience of some of the asylum-seeking children I've taught in Glasgow, it was important that Reema told her own story in her own words.

What are you hoping your reader will take away from the story?

I hope my novel will help readers to understand some of the issues faced by refugees and asylum seekers settling into a new country, as well as the problems that children here often struggle with: bullying, the loss of loved ones, and loneliness.

Despite the serious issues involved, Caylin and Reema's story is an adventure, and I'd like my readers to relate to these characters, and to feel invested in their quest to save the foxes and win their school a medal in the sports competition. I suppose the test of whether my book has had the intended impact on the reader is if they feel a little bit of the same sense of loss as I do when they reach the last page and find they've come to the end of Caylin and Reema's journey too.

Do you have any tips for people writing their own stories?

Write what excites you! A story takes a lot of time and work to get right, and if you're not fully invested in the world you've created and the characters who live there then it's much harder to resist the temptation to give up when the going gets tough. The first stories I wrote when I was five or six were (badly spelt!) retellings of films I'd seen, books my mother had read to me or cartoons I'd watched, and writing alternative plots to other people's stories can be a great way to get started, especially if it's a world you can really lose yourself in.

All writers begin as readers though, so read as many stories as you can and pay attention to the types of characters you identify with and the stories that move you or capture your imagination. If you can work out what makes you enjoy a story, then you'll find it much easier to write an adventure that your readers won't be able to put down.

If you enjoyed

The

FOX GIRL

and the

WHITE

GAZELLE

you might also
like these books...

Today's interesting events:

★ My sister explodes
🐚 I get a free holiday
🐚 I start hearing voices

Kelpies Prize Winner!

The Mixed-Up Summer of Lily McLean

Lindsay Littleson

Spend the summer with Lily McLean in this laugh-out-loud adventure

BRING YOUR IMAGINATION

THE NOWHERE EMPORIUM

ROSS MACKENZIE

The shop from nowhere can appear at any time, in any city. Its labyrinth of rooms contains wonders beyond belief.

But to enter you must pay a price.

Donald C...

Charles Tennant, Grey...

...m Cemetery

A ghostly lady in grey.
The paw prints of a gigantic hound.
With the help of his best friend Ham
boy-detective Artie Conan Doyle discovers
the secrets of the spooky Gravediggers' Club.

Can Artie solve
the mystery?

Or will his first
case be his last?

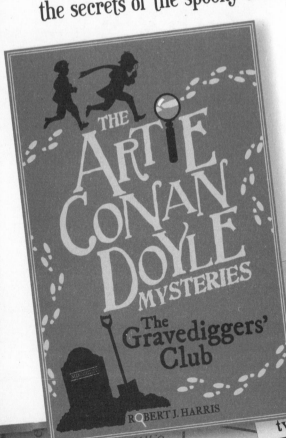

THE
ARTIE
CONAN
DOYLE
MYSTERIES

The
Gravediggers'
Club

ROBERT J. HARRIS

OBITUARY

Hamish Gowrie
...ed at the Grange C...
Saturday, Janua...
two o'clock in the a...
Friends and relativ...
deceased are cordia...